Mary Bassett Clarke

Autumn Leaves

Mary Bassett Clarke

Autumn Leaves

ISBN/EAN: 9783337362416

Printed in Europe, USA, Canada, Australia, Japan

Cover: Foto ©Andreas Hilbeck / pixelio.de

More available books at **www.hansebooks.com**

UTUMN
LEAVES

BY·

MARY BASSETT CLARKE
(IDA FAIRFIELD)

BUFFALO
CHARLES WELLS MOULTON
1895

PRINTED BY
CHARLES WELLS MOULTON,
Buffalo, N. Y.

CONTENTS.

LEGENDARY POEMS.

iv

RELIGIOUS POEMS.

MEMORIAL POEMS.

TEMPERANCE POEMS.

MISCELLANEOUS POEMS.

vi   CONTENTS.

LEGENDARY POEMS

LEGEND OF WATCH HILL.

WHERE the broad and solemn ocean
　　Laves the sandy shore,
Gently, when the tide is low,
And the waves in rhythmic flow,
Sigh along the strand,
Whispering, as they come and go,
Tales of other land,
Where the winds in wild commotion,
With a deafening roar
Dash the billows, mountain high,
Toward the cloud-encircled sky,
And the crests of snowy foam
Find on lofty rocks a home,
Vainly seeking thus to hide
Every brown and rugged side,
Towering in its grandeur still,
Stands the far-famed mound, Watch Hill.
Years and years ago, it stood
Thus serene beside the flood.
While, where now the golden grain
Waves upon the distant plain,
And the cottage gleaming white,
Greets the weary traveler's sight,
And the steepled church towers high,
With its Sabbath-pealing bell
Sounding warnings solemnly,
'Mid the organ's grandest swell;

Then the forests dark and wide
Stretching heavenward in their pride
Stood like brothers firm allied,
And the red-man's ear alone
Caught the solemn undertone,
Of the wild winds making moan.

Free as the wild deer of the woods,
Who roam through leafy solitudes,
In learning's ways untaught as they,
In pleasure rude, and fierce in play,
Vengeful in hate, with thirst for blood,
The war-like Pequots thronged the wood.
Learned the rude games their sires had taught
And boasted of the battles fought.
The scalp-locks hanging by his side
Awoke the warrior's fiercest pride,
Chased the young deer from hill to dale,
And made the antlered heroes quail,
And when the moonlight softly fell
On forest dark, and grassy dell,
With whoop and shriek of startling sound
Upon the smooth, untrodden ground,
In the wild war-dance, circled round.

But glimpses of a nobler race,
Amid this savage horde we trace,
Faint strivings of the deathless mind
Within such casket rude enshrined:
The stern heart, of the savage sire,
Was kindled with parental fire,
For the brave son, who bore his name,

And human love, and woe, the same
As to their pale-faced brothers came.
A wild, unfettered life, they shared,
The rude, unlettered path, prepared
By the Great-Spirit, for the feet
Which from the white man must retreat,
Forever backward, until lost
Along the wide, Pacific coast.

*   *   *   *   *   *

When the sun was shining brightly,
In the balmy month of June,
And the forest flowers were blooming,
And the forest birds in tune,
Down beside the sparkling water
At the noon of day,
With a tame fawn close beside her,
Gambolling in its play,
Came a maiden, Wahaneeta,
Daughter of the Pequot chief,
Bending low, she loosed her sandals,
With a smile of sweet relief,
As the salt wave sent its ripples
Softly o'er her slender feet,
Feet of such aerial lightness
That the waves in foamy whiteness
Gave them kisses sweet.
Fairest of the forest maidens,
Old Sassacus' pride.
Wahaneeta had been chosen
Many a warrior's bride,
But an answer, grave and tender,

On her sweet lips ready hung,
" Seek the brave some older maiden
Wahaneeta is too young,
Let her dwell with wise Sassacus,
Let her be her father's pride,
Years ago, beneath the hillock,
Laid the chieftain down his bride,
And his heart would grow too heavy,
And his tent too lonely be,
Ask her not to leave the chieftain,
Wahaneeta's heart is free."

Yet had eyes of radiant brightness,
Sometimes flashed upon her dreams,
.Gilding them with wondrous beauty
As the moonlight gilds the streams,
Eyes whose glances, dark and tender,
Flashed upon her path by day,
Till a maiden instinct warned her
She must turn her own away.
'Twas the young Manisses chieftain
Who had stirred her heart of late,
Once her nation's foe unconquered,
Object of her father's hate,
Though the hatchet now was buried
Though they hunted side by side,
Still her heart's misgivings taught her,
If the brave young warrior sought her,
She could never be his bride.

Wahaneeta on the sea-shore
With her playmate sported long.

Blending with the water's music,
Snatches of a wild, sweet song.
Till at last she weary grew;
To her side she gently drew
Her companion, as she sank
On the sea·grass, tall and rank
Which adorned the rugged bank.
Silently she watched the sunbeams
Which upon the waters lay,
Watched the golden, dancing sunbeams
With the laughing waves at play.
" Wahaneeta, Star of Beauty,"
Sang a low voice at her side,
" See, the warrior kneels before thee,
Wilt thou come, and be my bride ?

" Many braves has Shushuwanee,
Many scalps hang by his side,
Grave old sachems guide his councils,
Come, and be our nation's pride.
Turn not from me, Star of Beauty,
Listen to my spirit's cry,
Let me see thy smile of welcome,
Or in grief my heart will die,
Hear me, hear me, Wahaneeta,
Never maiden heard before
Shushuwanee pleading for her,
He can plead for thee no more."
Ceased the youthful chieftain's voice,
Waiting for the maiden's choice,
Would she yield her heart to one
Of a hated race the son ?

Wahaneeta saw undazzled,
Sunbeams glistening on the wave,
But she could not meet the glances
Of the young Manisses brave.
Memory of her father's hatred
Flashed across her troubled brain,
Hatred, which she knew unchanging,
Thrilled her heart with sudden pain,
Though that hatred seemed to sleep,
Still her father's heart must keep
Vengeful feelings buried deep.
But love's witchery o'er her stole,
Strangely thrilling all her soul,
Hope, in rainbow colors gay,
Decked the future of her way,
And her burning cheek was pressed
Closely to the warrior's breast,
While her whispering lips replied:
" I will be thine own true bride."

Silently the golden ray
From the waters died away,
Twilight gathered cold and gray;
Thus love's brightness would depart,
From the maiden's trusting heart,
Thus in sorrow, doubt and gloom,
Joy and life, find early tomb.
Soon a firm and heavy tread
Bade the maiden raise her head,
And love's raptured silence broke,
'Then a frown grew dark and low,
On Sassacus' haughty brow,

As the aged warrior spoke,
" Home, idle girl, thou long hast strayed,
Not thus, hast thou been taught,
Thy father's blanket still unmade,
His sandals yet unwrought."

Silently they stood before him,
Flushed with guilt and pride,
Wahaneeta would have hastened
From her lover's side,
But his gentle clasp detained her,
And his voice grew calm and clear,
With a conscious strength of purpose,
As he spake: " Brave warrior, hear,
Word for thee, has Shushuwanee,
'Tis a brave who asks of thee,
Give the maiden, Wahaneeta,
Let her go and dwell with me.
Far across the foaming waters
In the lodge beside the sea,
Loneliness and silence reigneth,
She will joy and gladness be,
There my braves await their chieftain,
They will greet with words of cheer,
True their arrows, swift their footsteps,
Foes, they never learned to fear,
Many skins for brave Sassacus,
Beads and wampum they shall bring,
For our tomahawk is buried,
And our warriors, now shall sing
But one song, around the camp-fire,
In the chilly winter's night,

' Brave Sassacus, wise in counsel,
Foremost in the fight.' "
Many shadows, swiftly changing,
Flitted o'er Sassacus' brow
As he heard the youthful chieftain
Speaking grave and low.
Grief and hate, together blending
With the cunning of his race,
Struggled fiercely in his bosom,
Shadowed dimly on his face.
But at length he schooled his features,
Calm his tone, and smooth his tongue:
" Let the warrior bide in patience,
Wahaneeta still is young,
Seek his home across the water,
Bring the bear-skins and the beads.
Bring the heavy belts of wampum,
Which the Pequot warrior needs,
See again Manisse maidens,
When three moons his love has tried,
If he seeks for Wahaneeta,
She shall be the chieftain's bride."
When the midnight moonlight, silvered
All the dew-bespangled dell,
And upon his couch of bear-skins,
Grim Sassacus slumbered well,
Wahaneeta heard the music
Of a wild, sweet, Indian lay,
"Rest thee, love, in sweetest slumber,
With the earliest dawn of day,
Shushuwanee hence must hasten,
Hasten on his watery way,

To the lodge of the Manisses,
To our ocean girdled isle,
All whose beauty yet shall blossom,
In the sunlight of thy smile.
Fear thou not, the swift-winged eagle
Soars not swifter toward the sun,
Than shall Shushuwanee hasten
Hither, when his task is done.
When the summer's sun shines hottest,
Wait thou, by the ocean's side,
Watch and wait for Shushuwanee,
He will come to claim his bride."
Swiftly sped the summer hours,
Bright with beauty, birds and flowers.
Wandering through the forest bowers,
Gathering many a bright-hued treasure,
Cast aside by careless wing
Of some rare bird, gay of plumage,
(Fit to ornament a king),
Weaving them in shapes fantastic
With gay quills of porcupine,
Fitting out her Indian wardrobe,
Wahaneeta passed the time.
But as warmer grew the sunbeams
In the sultry August days,
More she wandered by the sea-shore,
Singing still more joyous lays.
Looking often, toward the island,
With a bright, expectant face,
Donning every curious garment
Which could lend her added grace.
Growing restless, eager, anxious,

As the days passed one by one
And the youthful chieftain lingered
Still towards the setting sun.
Lingered did I say ? Poor maiden,
Little dreamed her trusting heart,
Of the secret foe, who followed,
With the swift and poisoned dart,
When her brave, young warrior started,
High with hopes, that dewy morn,
Hopes like dew-gems doomed to perish,
Soon of life and beauty shorn.
Scarce from Shushuwanee's vision
Had the Pequot lodges faded,
Scarcely hidden, was the shelter
Which his heart's best treasure shaded,
Floating still along the shore,
Rocking in his birch canoe,
When the poisoned arrow reached him,
Silent, swift and true.
For Sassacus' stealthy cunning,
Sent the treacherous spy,
In advance, to watch the chieftain,
And in ambush lie.
And the arrow found its victim,
And the life-blood of the brave,
In a dark, ensanguined current,
Tinged the briny wave.
Summer waned to gorgeous autumn,
And the balmy air
Shed a hazy, softened splendor
O'er the landscape fair.
Wahaneeta with that shadow,

Wan and shadowy grew,
Hope deferred a patient sorrow
O'er her spirit threw.
Daily, hourly now, her station
Was beside the sea,
Watching, waiting, looking sadly,
Where his bark should be.
Old Sassacus' brow grew sterner,
Sadder grew his heart,
Conscience sometimes smote him sorely,
For his treacherous part,
As he loved his gentle daughter
Fondly, as his nature knew,
And to win her back to pleasure
Would have brought to life anew,
The brave warrior, from the shadows
Of the far-off hunting ground,
But remorse or grief called vainly,
And the dead gave back no sound.
One by one the hues of autumn,
Changed to sober brown,
And the dead leaves of the forest,
One by one, came rustling down.
And the winds grew wild and chilly,
Sighing with a mournful tone,
Through the dreary, woodland mansions,
Like a broken spirit's moan.
Wahaneeta kept her station,
Still more frail and sad,
Heeding not her father's counsel,
Grief had made her mad.
Morn and evening, storm and sunshine,

E'en the lightning's glare
Found her watching still the ocean,
Watching, waiting there.
When the wild winds of November,
Swept the hillside long,
On the frosty breath of midnight,
Rose her mournful song:
" Thou art coming, I behold thee
Floating in thy bark canoe
Long for thee I've watched and waited,
To my promise true,
But the loneliness is passing,
Thou art hastening to my side.
Soon with joy and love unchanging
I shall be thine own true bride."

* * * * * *

With the morning's light, they found her,
Silent, cold and dead,
While the damp snow falling round her,
Robe of purest beauty spread.
'Neath the mound upon the hillock
Where her mother long had slept,
Old Sassacus gently laid her,
Silent, turned away and wept,
Colder, sterner grew his nature,
Deeper furrows on his brow,
As the years in sorrow lingered,
Till death's archer laid him low.
Time has swept from hill and forest,
Of the red man, every trace,
And the ancient haunts are peopled,

By a wiser, nobler race.
But the name of Wahaneeta,
Like sweet music lingers still,
Nature's tribute to affection,
And the mound is called Watch Hill.

CHARACTER.

TWO spirits, lately freed from earth,
    With strong impulsive force,
Through vast and trackless realms of space,
    Began their viewless course.
Each had his purpose well defined
    While dwelling here below,
And sped, like arrow tow'rd its mark
    Sent by unerring bow.

With each across the boundless waste,
    His guardian angel went,
And semblance of companionship
    Along the journey lent,
For there, as here, each spirit held
    His individual way
To realms of darker midnight still
    Or bright and brighter day.

The first beheld, and lo ! afar
    Uprose across his path
A form most horrible to view
    A shape of dread and wrath—

A demon of such frightful mein
  The gazer shrank in fear—
"Nay," said his angel, "wherefore shrink
  From what dost there appear?

" 'Tis but thyself, as thou wilt be
  When thou hast reached that line,
The future springs to meet thy gaze
  And show thee what is thine.
Long years ago, this selfsame path
  Thy feet commenced to tread;
And when yon state thou hast attained
  The goal lies far ahead."

The other saw, in distance far,
  A vision wond'rous fair,
A form of light, a saintly face,
  Clear eyes and shining hair,
A spirit of such loveliness
  He questioned with delight,
" And may I join yon seraph form,
  And walk with him in white?"

His angel smiling, answered him,
  "Thou but beholdest there,
Projected on the future's wall
  The form which thou wilt wear;
And still, while endless ages roll,
  Thou wilt approach to share
The glory of the Holy One,
  The Lord, beyond compare."

Oh ! solem Future, on thy scroll
   What pictures will appear,
In varying shades, intenser grown,
   With each succeeding year ?
Since time, its swift gradations here
   Seeks vainly to conceal,
What growth in good or evil, must
   Eternity reveal !

THE BEAUTIFUL TEMPLE.

IN far-off India, home of art,
   A costly temple stands,
So rarely beautiful, its name,
Is wafted on the wings of fame,
   A model for all lands.

But not alone in carven wood,
   Is wrought the wondrous spell ;
The pilgrim scents a sweet perfume,
Like breath of roses in their bloom,
   O'er beds of asphodel,

And peers in every shaded nook,
   The secret spell to know—
To find the alabaster vase,
Or incense-burning altar trace
   Or censer swinging low.

But naught discerns save works of art
   Produced with nicest care,
The painter's dream, the poet's thought,
In forms exquisitely enwrought,
   And beauty everywhere,

And fails perchance at last, to learn
   The secret hidden there,
In massive walls of odorous wood,
Which skillful workmen found so good
   To build the palace fair.

In silent grandeur towering high,
   The sun's first kiss to win,
No sign or token doth it bear,
Save witness of the perfumed air,
   That fragrance dwells within.

Like that grand temple is the life,
   With Christ indwelling there,
Whose quiet goodness, hour by hour,
Like odorous wood, or fragrant flower,
   With sweetness fills the air.

Build then, oh! soul, thy temple build,
   Of that most precious wood,
Its walls of character shall rise
To catch the brightness of the skies,
   And Heaven pronounce it good.

BABY'S KISS.

TRAMP, tramp the soldiers,
  Marching down the street,
Steadily the drum call
  Fell with even beat!
On their way to Gettysburg
  Went the " boys in blue,"
Who would e'er return again
  None among them knew.

Where the light was brightest,
  Lanterns swinging high,
Clapped her hands a baby
  With a joyful cry;
Never to her vision
  Came so fair a sight,
Music, men and torches
  In the quiet night.

" Halt!" "the boys " were resting
  For a moment brief;
Foot-sore men, and weary,
  Glad of this relief.
Brighter seemed the pageant
  To the baby's eyes,
While she shouted louder
  In her sweet surprise.

" May I kiss the baby ? "
    Said a soldier near,
Brushing with his coat-sleeve
    From his cheek a tear;
" Just so fair another,
    Long, long months ago
Left I, in the homestead
    Where the north winds blow."

Lightly to his bosom
    Sprang the eager child,
Touched his rough cheek softly
    With her lips, and smiled.
All night long the soldier
    Felt the impress there,
Sweeter than the rose-leaf
    On the summer air.

Tenderly he placed her
    Back in mother's arms,
Home and country dearer
    For her baby charms:
Through the tiresome marches
    Walked with firmer tread,
For the brief enfolding
    Of that golden head.

Morning brought the battle:
    Fast the brave men fell,
Mown, like grass in summer,
    By the shot and shell.

Down amid the trenches
  Where the dead were piled,
Sleeps the gallant soldier,
  Far from wife and child. ·

HETTY MARVIN.

AN INCIDENT OF THE REVOLUTION.

SPREADING the linen beside the stream,
  Watching it bleach in the sun's bright gleam,
Sprinkling the water with small, white hand,
Fair as the fairest in all the land
Was Hetty Marvin, the little maid
Of twelve, who beside the linen staid.

Sweet Hetty Marvin, whose mother brave,
Good Governor Griswold's head to save,
When the British attacked New London town
And many a patriot brave shot down,
Her cousin had safely hidden away,
In her quiet home, for many a day.

But winds had wafted the secret back,
And the subtile foe were on his track.
A price was set on the Governor's head,
And for further safety, again he fled
With rapid footsteps across the way,
Where Hetty bleached her linen that day.

He paused a moment beside the maid,
" My life is in danger grave," he said,
" I hasten to reach my little boat,
Below on the stream it is now afloat,
But say to the British when they reach here,
That I took the other path, my dear."

"Nay," said the little maiden, "nay,
You must not ask me to do that way,
Why do you tell me which way you go,
When I should not tell a lie, you know?"
And yielding at once to her anxious fears,
Poor Hetty burst in a flood of tears.

The Governor spake with bated breath:
" Would you give your cousin away to death,
My only hope is to turn them back,
Their search to make on another track,
So tell them I fled by the other way,
And Heaven will bless you many a day."

The Puritan maiden quickly replied,
"Heaven would not bless me, if I lied,
But though they kill me, they shall not know
From me, the direction which you go,
But stay, good cousin, why further fly?
Hide under my web, which is spread to dry.

Quick, I will cover you safely o'er,
And sprinkle my linen as before."
There was little time to discuss the plan,
Less chance of safety if on he ran

For over the hill at once they knew
A band of Tories appeared in view.

The party halted beside the maid,
The voice of the leader roughly said:
"Child, have you seen a man to-day,
Running as if for life away?"
Poor little Hetty paled with fear,
But answered "Yes" in a voice quite clear.

"Which way did he go?   Now answer well,"
Said Hetty: "I promised not to tell,"
"You shall," screamed the leader with an oath,
"Or soon by Heaven I'll hang you both."
But Hetty sobbed: "I have promised fair,
That though you killed me, I'd not tell where."

Then another spake in a voice more mild
"This is Hetty Marvin, I know the child,
This man is your mother's cousin, dear,
We are friends of his, so you need not fear,
But what did he say?   Tell us all you can
We can help him more, if we know his plan."

Now Hetty was not at all deceived,
But answered as though she at once believed,
"He said he desired to reach his boat,
Which down the river was then afloat,
But wanted me, when you came, to say
That he had gone up the other way."

"Why didn't you answer as you were told,
When I asked you?" thundered the leader bold,
"Good sir, I could never tell a lie,"
Said Hetty, wiping a tearful eye,
"Then tell me truly," the Tory said
"What were his parting words, good maid?"

So Hetty answered, with half a frown
"His only chance was to hasten down,
He said," and trembling still with fright,
She hid her face in her apron white,
They fancied there was no need to stay,
And the British tories rode away.

When night her mantel of darkness spread,
O'er hill and valley and river bed,
The boat was signalled again to shore,
And the Governor floated swiftly o'er,
To a shelter safe, where he well might bless
His shrewd little cousin's truthfulness.

WINGLESS BIRDS.

THERE is an ancient legend,
  A myth of many words,
Which tells us the Creator
  When he had formed the birds,
Laid down their wings beside them
  And said: "Your burdens know,
Take up, and bear them bravely,
  And you shall stronger grow."

They lifted them and bound them
  One upon either side,
A burden great and heavy,
  They could not seek to hide:
They held them close and bore them
  As something wisely sent,
While forth to do life's duties
  In cheerfulness they went.

Time passed, and they no longer
  With halting steps must run,
But borne on strong, swift pinions
  They soared to meet the sun:
They soared and sang together
  Above their low estate,
Uplifted by the burdens
  Which once had seemed so great.

May we not learn the lesson
Of sorrow sent in love?
Of burdens which shall lift us
As wings bear up the dove?
Of trials changed to triumphs
Along the path we trod
Which kept our feet from straying,
And drew us nearer God?

Then shrink not from the sorrow,
The burden bravely bear,
By faith and patience girded,
Thou shalt not know despair,
The sorrow, though so crushing,
The burden, though so great
On eagle's wings shall bear thee
To reach thy high estate.

THE PILGRIMS.

A BAND of pilgrims came one day,
All bowed and wrinkled, worn and gray,
Beside an ancient shrine to pray.

A sacred shrine, which seemed to stand
A lonely landmark in the land,
By purest breezes gently fanned.

From crowded cities far apart,
Or noisy streets or busy mart,
Yet held in many a loyal heart.

Back from its base uprose the hills,
Whose calm, majestic grandeur thrills
The spirit, and with rapture fills.

The wide, cool meadows stretched below,
Whose peaceful beauty seemed to glow,
Through summer's green or winter's snow.

And all about the hallowed spot,
On sunny slopes or shaded grot,
Bloomed out the blue forget-me-not.

Together, clasping hand in hand,
In silence knelt that pilgrim band,
With faces bowed toward the sand.

Then suddenly, o'er each one fell
A weird enchantment, like a spell,
With visions which no tongue can tell.

And backward swept the tide of years,
Concealing all life's cares and fears,
Its disappointments, sorrows, tears.

And gliding through the sunset's glow,
Advanced with stately steps and slow,
The loved, of fifty years ago.

As through the moonlight stars appear,
So one by one, to each drew near
The face, once held, of all most dear.

Not all were lover's faces true,
For some had lost the morning dew
Of youth and beauty, ever new.

But each, in that dim long-a-go
Had held supremest place, and lo!
Each stood transfigured in the glow.

The years were naught, whose toil and care
Had furrowed cheeks, once smooth and fair,
And bleached to snow, the darkest hair.

It mattered not, that most were laid,
Long years before, beneath the shade
The lilies of the valley made.

Fresh as the dawn, and fair and sweet,
With shining eyes, and noiseless feet,
They came, the early loved to greet.

Then hope revived, where hope was dead,
And joy returned, where joy had fled,
And youth crowned every hoary head.

Not to the outer world displayed
The peace, which on the soul was laid
By quickened pulses half betrayed.

But they who went their separate ways,
With grateful hearts gave God the praise,
Strengthened for many coming days.

And turning from the hallowed place,
Went forth with added joy and grace,
· Love's glory shining in each face.

PERFECTION.

SUMMONED before their mighty king,
    The cunning workmen came,
The sculptors who for wondrous skill
    Had won immortal fame.

" Ye have done well," the monarch said,
    But much indeed remains,
For Art, through patient toil alone,
    Perfection e'er attains.

Not simple good, perfection now
    Your lawful sovereign claims,
Go forth, and labor for this end,
    Content with no low aims.

Bring me the finished work your hands
    Through faithful years have wrought,
The faultless marble, by your skill
    To full perfection brought."

Forth from the presence of their king,
   The workmen slowly passed,
With silent tongues and clouded brows
   And spirits overcast,

But murmured when among themselves,
   "In vain our skill or strength,
What shall it profit that we toil
   For years, to fail at length ?

" No perfect work hath mortal hand
   E'er wrought beneath the sun,
And farther from our grasp it seems,
   Than when we first begun."

But one (a loyal, loving heart,
   Though humble) made reply,
"Our master hath commanded us,
   Indeed, we can but try."

Then earnestly his task begun,
   And diligently wrought,
While day by day, in beauty grew
   The marvel which he sought.

But to his practised eye, defects,
   By others passed unseen,
Appeared his work to mar, and rose
   His hope and him between.

And when his years of toil were passed,
 And he was called to bring
His statue for the king's delight,
 He came but sorrowing.

" Dear master, I have tried," he said,
 " The best my hand can do
Demands but pardon for its faults,
 My gracious king, from you."

The monarch smiled approvingly,
 And touched the polished stone,
When lo! the chiseled form at once,
 With full perfection shone.

Thus vainly, through the years we strive,
 A character to bring,
Of faultless symmetry to Him,
 Our well-beloved King.

By evil marred, through stains of sin
 Its beauties dimly shine,
And evermore perfection waits
 The touch of the Divine.

BESSIE.

AN INCIDENT OF THE WAR OF THE REBELLION.

SHE stood by the President's elbow—
　　" Well, what do you want, my child?"
Said the busy, good man, gravely,
　　As he lifted his eyes and smiled.

" My brother," half-whispered Bessie,
　" He is to be shot to-day,
I have come to beg for his pardon,
　　You will not send me away?"

"Your brother? Ah! yes, I remember,
　I am sorry it must be so,
But a thousand lives were endangered,
　　He slept at his post, you know.

"And this is a time of trouble,
　You scarcely can understand,
The dead and the dying are many,
　　And sorrow all over the land."

" He slept, but only a moment,
　He had marched all day, you know,
And carried his comrade's knapsack,
　　With his, through the mud and snow.

"And it was'nt his night to be sentry,
　But his comrade felt so bad,
He thought him quite to ill to stand,
　So he took his place, poor lad.

" He never knew how it happened,
　He meant to have kept awake,
He wrote all about it to papa,
　And the letter, please, you may take."

The President read the letter,
　Tears brimming his clear, gray eyes,
And said, "why, the boy is a hero,
　And worthy to win a prize.

" The boy who could write such a letter,
　So honest and full of good-will,
So loyal to country and comrade—
　That country has need of him still."

He hurriedly scribbled a message,
　And sent with the greatest speed—
A message of peace and pardon
　To one in the sorest need.

And turning to still, tearful Bessie,
　His hand lightly laid on her head—
"Be patient, my little one, waiting,
　Your brother is safe now," he said.

"Rest here, in my quietest corner,
  Be happy, the hours will be few,
And when you return home this evening,
  Your brother shall go with you."

Curled up on the President's sofa,
  Who gentlest watch over her kept,
Amid the affairs of the nation,
  The little girl quietly slept.

When night spread her shadowy curtain,
  The moon and the stars looking down
Saw the child and her soldier brother,
  Fast speeding away from the town.

And through the long, terrible conflict,
  No friends of the Union more true
Than Bessie, whose love saved her brother,
  And her brother, who still wore the blue.

SEVEN WISE MEN.

HAVE you heard of "seven wise men of Greece,"
    And the legend strange if true,
Of the golden tripod in their nets,
    Some fishers, fishing drew?
The golden tripod cast away,
    By the hand of Helen fair,
Who sailed from Troy, long years ago,
    In sorrow and dispair.

Have you heard that as they drew their net,
    And thus the prize obtained,
They quarreled, each with each, to know
    Who had the treasure gained?
And they brought the mystic, golden seat,
    To the temple, quaint and old,
Of the Archer-god, for light and law,
    The priestess might unfold.

"To the wisest man throughout all Greece,
    You shall give," the priestess said—
So to Bias, famed for learning great,
    The seat at once was sped.
But the old Greek savan stoutly claimed
    That another was more wise,
And only Solon, he declared,
    In truth could claim the prize,

To the wisest seven men, it passed,
  And they each and all disclaimed
The right, to own the precious gift,
  Or to be for wisdom famed.
And again the fishers in dispair
  To the temple, bore the seat,
Where it found a quiet resting-place
  At the great Appolo's feet.

And for years, that voiceless oracle,
  To the world, the lesson taught
That the wisest ever humblest are,
  While fools are found unsought.
And still the truth remains unchanged,
  For the wise of every age
Are the unpretending of their class,
  Whether scholar, priest or sage.

ELIAB.

COMMUNING with his own great heart,
  Eliab thought to dwell apart
From others, filling all his days,
With sacrifice of prayer and praise.

Learned in all wisdom of the wise,
Possessing wealth he well might prize,
His sated soul grew dark within
By pondering on earth's wrong and sin.

" This life is worthless all, and vain,
My heart is sick with bitter pain "
He said. " The ages that have been,
Like this dark age, are full of sin.

" I care not longer to behold,
The wretchedness the years enfold,
Men toil and struggle, strive and cry,
Availing nought ! I would but die,"

An aged priest, a holy man,
Discerning dimly God's great plan,
An herb of healing brought, and laid
Upon Eliab's palm and said:

" Brother beloved, go forth, and bear
This herb of healing virtues rare,
To wreched homes.   When seven men
Are healed, I'll come to thee again."

Eliab turned his steps within
The homes of misery and sin,
Where poverty and crime and pain,
On human hearts left darkest stain.

And as he went from door to door,
His wealth bore comforts to the poor,
The ignorant his wisdom learned,
The sad to him for solace turned.

The sick rejoiced in health anew,
The friendless in a friend so true,
But when were healed the seven men,
The priest sought Eliab again.

"I bring to thee the herb of death,
Since thou art weary of thy breath,"
He said, "for heaven has heard thy cry,
And if thou wilt, thou may'est die."

"Nay, God forbid!" Eliab cried,
"It shames me that I would have died,
Ere kindly deed my hand had done,
Or life worth living had begun. ,

"The way so dark, grows bright to me,
Life's use and meaning now I see.
Who loves and seeks to do God's will,
Must love and serve his brother still.

"Reach other lives, with outstretched hand
Lift up the fallen, help them stand,
Put selfish joy and ease aside
To save the souls for whom Christ died."

THE WHITE ELEPHANT.

LONG years ago the Hindoos say
    Wise Buddha walked the earth
Slow-paced and strong, with velvet feet,
A life sustained and calm and sweet
    But not of human birth.

Submitted to the hand of man,
    As one of humbler state,
With patience bore the whip and thong,
In silence suffered scorn and wrong,
    Thus growing truly great.

And when the wheel of fate revolved
    He came to earth again,
A princely soul, in princely form,
With heart most loving, true and warm,
    A blessing to all men.

The beauty of self-sacrifice
    For other's good, he taught,
The peace which patience may attain,
The strength and sweetness born of pain,
    The joy of service wrought.

Though fatal errors marred his creed,
Enough of truth remained
To write, as with an iron pen,
For ages on the hearts of men,
The lesson it contained.

And still his million votaries
With pious awe adore
The form, tradition makes his own,
Wherein he walked the earth unknown,
As sacred evermore.

THE OLD CLOCK'S STORY.

A HUNDRED years I have stood by the wall,
So dark and massive, solemn and tall,
To tell the old, how the years go by,
To tell the young, how the moments fly,
And ticking, ticking, steadily, slow,
Have swung my pendulum to and fro.

My face is yellowed and marred and old,
My hands are dull, which have been like gold,
My voice rings out, as it did in youth,
And still I am able to tell the truth,
A valued gift, which I must confess,
Some clocks and men, do not now possess.

My maker, owner, was tall and slim,
And fine of features, and strong of limb,
A skillful workman, an honest man
Who fashioned me on the self-same plan.
Ah! me, the changes which I have seen,
For fifty years has his grave been green.

It seems but a day, since full of grace,
He brought his bride to behold my face;
She smiled on me with a child's delight
And touched my hands with her own, so white,
She sang my praisies from year to year,
And never a word of blame would hear.

The time passed on and the children came,
A noisy group. I could call by name,
Six noble sons, who to manhood grew,
They loved me well and each other too,
I ticked my warning and tried to save,
But one went down to a drunkard's grave.

Four beautiful girls were my delight,
So healthy, happy, rosy and bright,
They worked and romped and chatted and sang,
The plain old rooms with their music rang,
They heard my call, with the morning's light,
They said their prayers in my ears at night.

And one by one, they blossomed and grew
To lovely womanhood pure and true,
And one by one, they went forth to shine
In homes still brighter and fairer than mine,

Till only the youngest remained to bless
A mother's heart with her fond caress.

Too well I remember the sorrowful hour,
When sickness blighted our beautiful flower,
I watched her cheek with its fever stain,
And hushed my voice to lighten her pain,
The flying moments I strove to stay,
To lengthen the life fast ebbing away.

But all in vain, for they bore her away,—
The sun seemed darkened for many a day,
My voice rang strangely amid the gloom,
The quiet house and the lonely room,
The listening mourners sadly said
" The old clock's tolling for the dead."

The years rolled on, I sounded their knell,
At last in flames the old house fell,
But I was saved to a happier fate,
Still ticking the moments early and late,
To link with memory's golden chain
The buried past and the present again.

And still I am standing, stately and tall,
But polished anew for the newer hall,
A family relic, cherished with pride,
The grandchildren's children throng my side,
And listen and call in accents sweet,
To hear the story which I repeat.

THE CLAY SPARROW.

A LEGEND.

HAVE you ever heard the story
　　Which old Icelanders tell,
A legend of the Christ-child
　　Who used on earth to dwell ?
How that, playing with his comrades
　　One sunny, summer's day,
They fashioned little sparrows,
　　From soft and yielding clay.

And perchance, they blocked the side-walk,
　　(As little children will,)
In eager zeal to cherish
　　Such tokens of their skill,
For a dignified old Rabbi
　　Swept grandly by the place,
And scattered all their treasures,
　　With scorn upon his face.

All the little birds were broken
　　And cast into the street,
Where sure destruction waited,
　　Beneath the passer's feet,
And the children fell to grieving,
　　With angry words and noise,
And sobs of real sorrow,
　　Above their broken toys.

Then the heart of the Child-Jesus,
  By tender pity stirred,
Awoke in sweet compassion
  As he their sorrow heard,
And filled with power unconscious,
  With gesture of command
Above the broken fragments
  He waved his childish hand.

And behold, a wondrous marvel,
  Which every tear might dry,
Each little bird flew singing
  And soaring to the sky;
For the lifeless clay was quickened,
  By his unuttered thought,
Who woke the worlds to being,
  And earth from chaos brought.

Now we do not think this legend
  Is like our scriptures true,
But there are greater marvels
  Which our good Christ can do.
For the spirits marred and broken,
  The hearts all stained with sin,
He changes to his likeness,
  And sets his peace within.

And at last, when these frail bodies
  Have lived their little day,
And touched by the Destroyer
  Shall fall like broken clay,

At the voice of this dear Saviour
   The spirits shall arise
And robed in life immortal,
   Soar heavenward through the skies.

SI-LING

OR THE RADIANT ONE.

'TIS the Chinese tell the story,
   Of a spirit wondrous fair,
Who once left her home in glory,
   Earthly wants and woes to share,
Came and dwelt with royal Hwong-Ti,
   As the empress of the land;
But no selfish empress was she,
   Thus to rule with idle hand.

Not to be a stately lily,
   In the royal, ivory chair,
But to help the poor, who illy
   All their griefs and burdens bear;
And the sick and heavy-hearted
   To make glad with hope and peace
While the dying ones departed
   Full of joy at their release.

And she taught the art of spinning
   Silks and wools of brilliant dyes,
With her own deft fingers winning,
   For the richest robe, the prize.

Taught the dignity of labor,
  For the rich as well as poor,
Thus to help each humble neighbor
  Every burden to endure.

But alas! for human nature,
  There were envious, then as now,
There were jealous, who would hate her
  Nor to her mild scepter bow;
'Till at length, her purest action
  Became subject, in their eyes,
For suspicion and detraction,
  And she sought again the skies.

Thus she left them, but the treasure
  Of her noble life remained,
Freely given without measure
  Was the good they had obtained;
For the useful arts still flourish,
  Which her skillful hand supplied,
And the mulberry was nourished
  With the tea-plant, side by side.

From the " Kingdom of the Sages,"
  With their legend lore enwrought,
Ever brighter through the ages
  Shines the truth our Saviour taught,—
That the life of high or lowly
  May be purer than earth's pelf,
And the sacrifice most holy
  Is the sacrifice of self.

THE MOSS ROSE.

THERE is an old, sweet story told,
  No doubt you've heard the same,
To minister to human needs,
  An angel earthward came,
And, wearied, lay one summer's day
  Beneath the rose tree's shade;
To win refreshment from fatigue,
  His lengthened journey made.

With soothing spell the shadows fell,
  And restful coolness lent,
While gentle slumbers o'er him stole
  With sweetest odors blent—
Refreshed he rose, and for repose
  His gratitude to prove,
Desired some parting gift to leave
  In token of his love.

The rose replied, with an air of pride,
  "Your wondrous powers I know—
From out your boundless stores on me
  Another grace bestow."
With smiling face, in swift embrace,
  The angel nearer drew,
And o'er each stem and bud and bloom
  A veil of moss he threw.

The charm it lent, the lesson meant,
  Is free to great and small—
That beauty should be lowly still,
  For God bestoweth all.
Then let us pore this legend o'er
  And of its good take part,
The added grace we ever need
  Is humbleness of heart. ·

THE TRUE CROSS.

'TIS said, the mother—wise and good—
  Of Constantine the Great,
Bent on a pious pilgrimage,
  Once left her high estate,
And through the paths of Palestine
  Wandered with weary feet,
Searching for tokens of her Lord
  The unfamiliar street;

And grieved to note, how time and man
  Had swept, with ruthless hand,
The frail memorials of his love
  From that once favored land.
Yet found, amid the debris, where
  Tradition marked his doom,
Three crosses, rude reminders left
  Of hour of darkest gloom.

But which the sacred wood, whereon
  Her bleeding Savior died?
" How shall I know the true and false?"
  In bitterness she cried.
Ere long, from one, such healing power
  As every doubt removed,
Revealed His touch, who, living still,
  The great physician proved.

Oh! Christian mothers, everywhere,
  Who seek the good and true—
The legend of the healing cross
  Its lesson has for you.
The patient, faithful mother's love,
  By long night-watches tried,
Through time and change, unchanging still,
  In blessings shall abide.

The healing touch of tender hands
  Which soothed the brow of pain,
The balm of cheering words, which fell
  Like showers of summer rain—
These shall their own rich fruitage bear,
  Through time and change and loss;
And unto watchful eyes reveal
  Life's dearest, holiest cross.

THE COMMON LOT.

A WEEPING woman, so the Hindoos say,
    Half-crazed with grief, to Buddha came one day,
        And cried in accents wild,
     "Oh! bring to life my child,
      My boy, my only one,
      Who died at set of sun.

"For thou, oh! holy prophet, thou hast power
To bring again to life this faded flower.
        Wilt thou not heal this pain,
        These tears which fall like rain,
        This heart bereft of joy?
        Oh! give me back my boy!"

Then long and pityingly the prophet gazed
Upon the stricken form, and gently raised
        The drooping, grief-bowed head,
        As tenderly he said,
     "Aye, thou shalt find relief
     And solace for thy grief.

"Go forth, my daughter, 'mid the homes of men,
And when thy task is done, return again,
        Bringing black mustard seed—
        Fruit of a pungent weed—
        Gathered, it matters not,
       'n palace or in cot,

"So that thou bring it, from the favored home,
Into whose circle death has never come.
      This trophy bring to me,
      And thou shalt surely see,
      From the mist-shrouded shore,
      Thy lost return once more."

Forth went the mother on her eager quest,
Sped North and South, and hurried East and West,
      In every home she stood,
      As one who begs for food,
    "Oh! give me, in my need,
      One grain of mustard seed,

" And I will bear it to the prophet wise,
For he with it can open death-sealed eyes.
      Kind friends, are ye all here,
      Father and mother dear,
      And wife and child and slave ?
      For only thus 'twill save."

The poor are pitiful, and everywhere
They freely offered of their store a share,
      But answered with a tear,
    " Nay, death is ever near,
      And many loved have flown,
      We wait almost alone.

" For earth is full of weariness and pain,
And he who sows the seed reaps not the grain,
      The wide world, with thy grief,
      Seeks vainly for relief,

And for thy human woe
Tears will forever flow."

Then slowly o'er her selfish sorrow rose
A tender pity for the great world's woes,
A patient, painless calm
Fell on her heart like balm,
And peace, God's peace, came down,
Her barren life to crown.

BY THE SEA.

"CITY OF WACO."

The steamship City of Waco, was burned off Galveston, November 8th, 1875. Every soul on board perished.

A BLACK and rayless night
 Hung o'er the deep its pall,
Moonless and starless stretched the sky,
 Its canopy o'er all.

The ships, which all day long
 Had sped, like swift-winged birds,
Rocked idly on the sullen waves,
 With sails by breeze unstirred.

The listening sailor heard
 Only the loon's wild cry,
Or sea-gull, shrieking to its mate,
 Lost in the darkness nigh.

The watching sailor saw
 Only the warning light
On distant headlands, gleaming o'er
 The rock-reefs sunk from sight.

But soon, athwart the sky,
 The forked lightnings flash,
And following swift, the thunders boom,
 And shake with sudden crash.

The winds responsive shriek,
  Or sob with mournful wail,
The waves in foaming fury rise,
  Lashed by the angry gale.

The ships plunge madly now,
  Their cables tug and strain,
As if the demons of the deep
  Strove hard to break the chain.

Oh! watchman, at your post,
  Amid this midnight storm,
What added terror pales your cheek
  And shakes your stalwart form?

Behold, a ship on fire!
  No timely warning came,
But swiftly deck and spar and mast
  Were wrapped in sheeted flame.

Tossed on the billows high,
  Plunged neath the foaming tide,
No floods the angry flames could quench,
  Nor could the waters hide.

High towering toward the sky,
  A vast funereal pyre,
The heavens their tears in torrents poured,
  But could not quench the fire.

No friendly arm could reach,
  No pitying hand could save—
A blazing star lit up the night,
  A meteor on the wave.

What of the human freight
  That good ship proudly bore ?
Hark! how the eager cry rings out
  From distant homes on shore.

What of the living souls
  Who went from homes of love,
And trusted that the winds and waves
  Would willing servants prove ?

Ask not the stormy wind,
  Ask not the hungry wave,
Though high the angry waters swept,
  And wide the yawning grave.

But ask that giant king
  Whose tongues of flame combine
To lap the salt waves from her deck,
  And drink her blood, like wine.

Who bars the cabin doors
  With flaming walls so high,
And smothers in his fiery arms
  Each anguish-riven cry.

Only the watchman saw,
  Amid the blinding storm,
Clinging to broken spar or mast,
  The wraith of human form.

Only the watchman heard,
  From out the storm and flame,
The voice of those who cried for help,
  For help which never came.

The grasping sea gave back
  To those who watched it well,
Of all who knew the fearful tale,
  No living tongue to tell.

Only the blackened forms
  The furnace could not melt;
Only the marred and ruined shrines,
  Where love and joy once dwelt.

The morning rose at last,
  Serenely still and fair;
The Storm-King, vanquished for the time,
  Crept to his hidden lair.

The sun revealed his face
  O'er distant hill-tops bright,
The sea, repentant, wept her tears
  In rainbow hues of light.

And thus, in Heaven's clear light,
  Earth's shadows flee away,
And thus shall dawn, on death's dark night,
  Immortal life's pure day.

SEA DREAMS.

ON a lone rock beside the sea
  I mused, and watched afar
The white-caps dashing in their glee
  Across the sandy bar.

Beside me stretched the long, low shore
  Where sand and ocean meet ;
The waves rolled in with ceaseless roar,
  And broke beneath my feet.

Across the far horizon lay
  A gold and crimson sky ;
The cloud-robes, which the dying day,
  Departing, had cast by.

Slow-sailing ships before me passed,
  With white wings widely spread,
As silently as shadows cast
  By summer clouds o'erhead.

From East, from West, they nearer drew,
　And crossed before my sight,
Then noiseless faded from my view,
　Into the gathering night.

I thought, what isles of beauty wait
　Each vessel's devious way ;
What golden morns and sunsets late
　Shall gild each coming day.

What marts of trade, what ports of peace
　Their wings shall hover near ;
What gold and gems their wealth increase,
　What welcomes give them cheer.

Perchance, what unseen dangers hide,
　From which no skill can save ;
What wreck and ruin grimly ride
　Upon the storm-tossed wave.

Ah! me, how many yet will find
　In ocean depths a tomb,
Nor know the snares of fate unkind,
　Which drew them to their doom.

One little moment o'er their path
　I cast an anxious eye,
But know not what the future hath
　Of storm or sunny sky.

The sea spread wide her billowy waste,
　The genii of the night
Its pall of darkness drew in haste,
　To shut them from my sight.

Thus life spreads out, through winding ways,
　Whose end I can not see ;
In vain I seek, with longing gaze,
　To scan eternity!

Oh! mystery of the unseen world,
　　Thy cloudy curtains fall,
Like banners by the breeze unfurled,
　To shut my gaze from all—

From all which lies before, beyond—
　A vast, unsounded sea,
Whose depths of mystery profound,
　Still tempt and trouble me.

Oh! wondrous future! when unrolled,
　Shall thy deep waters flow
O'er beds of pearl and sands of gold ?
　Or rocky reefs of woe ?

What ships, which speed time's billows o'er,
　With favoring wave and wind,
Stranded upon a wreck-strewn shore,
　Some coming morn shall find ?

What ships by wildest storms distressed,
   Beyond earth's changing tide,
Shall, 'mid the islands of the blest,
   In peaceful harbor ride?

Alas! the night has darker grown,
   One star alone gives light,
We journey toward the great Unknown
   By faith and not by sight.

Yet, while life's evening shadows fall,
   May we not trust His love,
Who will, through storms and darkness all,
   Our faithful Pilot prove?

THE LIGHT-HOUSE.

A LONG, low range of dangerous rocks,
   Oft hidden by the tide,
Well nigh two centuries ago,
   Were made the sailor's guide;
A massive light-house rose thereon,
   Whose welcome beams shone far,
When midnight darkness veiled from sight
   The friendly moon and star.

Who built at first, his structure reared
   With patient skill and care,
And decorative art invoked,
   To make it grand and fair.

But when the storm-king, in his wrath,
   To fierce destruction moved,
The balconies which lent such grace,
   Its utter ruin proved.

Another built with wiser thought,
   Cast ornament aside,
Nor trick of foolish fancy brought,
   To catch the wind and tide—
A granite tower, whose strength defied
   Alike the sea and wind,
But lined with wood, and doomed therefrom
   A fiery death to find.

Yet from its ashes, Phœnix-like,
   The light-house rose once more
In soolemn grandeur, statelier far,
   More perfect than before.
By failure taught, the architect
   This lesson learned with care,
That only excellence the test
   Of centuries will bear.

THE FISHERMAN.

THE fisherman rocks in his shell of a boat,
 The fisherman sturdy and brave,
And day after day, on the ocean afloat,
 He rides on the foam-crested wave.

And sometimes he carries a tiny white sail,
 And sometimes he bends to the oar,
And often is borne on the breath of the gale
 His song floating back to the shore.

The fisherman's wife in the cottage sits down,
 With her little brown babe on her knee,
And sometimes she glances with smile or with frown
 On the children who sport by the sea;

But often she turns with a far-reaching gaze,
 To the distant dim speck on the wave,
The treacherous wave which so often betrays
 And proves but the fisherman's grave.

The children climb up on the rocks in the sand,
 And wait for the incoming tide,
All ready and eager, with basket in hand,
 The fisherman spoils to divide.

And never a charm doth the fisherman lack
 To capture the shy, shining fish,
He trolls and he angles for blue and for black,
 And lands them alike in his dish.

To the fishers of old, came the Savior of men,
   As they mended their nets by the sea,
He called to them tenderly, once and again,
   " Leave them all, and come, follow thou me."

The fishermen still hear his voice by the sea,
   For he speaks to them ever as then,
"Come follow ye me my diciples to be
   And ye shall be fishers of men."

LIIVING WATERS.

A TALE is told of a ship which lay
   Becalmed at sea on a sultry day,
With idle sails, and a thirsting crew,
Benumbed and faint, with a terror new.

For wind and wave had conspired to show,
Their journey long and their progress slow,
But stormy sea or the tempest's breath
Was naught, compared to this dreadful death.

Their way was lost on the pathless sea,
And still far off must the harbor be,
But lo! a sail in the distance shone,
A steamship sped o'er the path unknown.

It nearer drew, as they hoping gazed;
The captain stood with his trumpet raised,
" Ho! ship ahoy!" was his eager cry,
" Give us some water, or else we die."

No answer came to his call at first,
" Ho! ship ahoy! must we die of thirst?
We perish here in this briny sea,
Draw near and give of your store to me."

Then backward came the reply so clear,
" The mouth of the Amazon is here,
So drop your buckets, both great and small,
And fill, for water is free to all."

How oft, adrift on life's changing sea,
And parched with thirst, like that crew, are we,
For storms have driven us from our way,
Or calms delayed, and afar we stray.

The broken cisterns, so poor and small,
Wherefrom we drank, have been emptied all,
Till each sad heart lifts at last the cry,
" Lord, save in pity, or else I die."

How welcome, then, is the voice we hear,
" The fount of joy is forever near,
Salvation spreads like a mighty sea,
And living streams are awaiting thee."

"THE SEA ·IS HIS."

I WANDER on the pebbly strand,
  Beneath my feet is yielding sand,
Before me stretches, vast and grand,
  The ocean with incoming tide,
Whose foam-capped billows o'er and o'er,
Dash on the rocks with deaf'ning roar,
And break and die along the shore,
  My faltering steps beside.

And thus, for age on age untold,
O'er granite rocks or sands of gold,
The ocean's flowing tides have rolled,
  Nor ever ceased to rise and fall.
Held in the hollow of his hand,
Who holds the worlds, at whose command,
From chaos sprang both sea and land,
  Obedient to His call.

A thousand years are in his sight
But as the watches of a night,—
A foam-flash on the waters bright,—
  Or sunset's golden afterglow.
Ten thousand years, still undismayed,
The sea His mandate has obeyed,
" And here shall thy proud waves be stayed,
  No further shalt thou go."

Empires have held their mighty sway,
Nations have grown and passed away,
Man is the creature of a day,
   With all his power and pride,
How brief the measure of his years,
How trivial his hopes and fears,
How small his puny strength appears,
   The ocean depths beside.

In silence sleep the great of old,
The giants of the past, so bold,
Their race is run, their tale is told,   '
   They lie with folded hands,
And sealed lips and quiet breast,
And brown earth-mold above them pressed,
For centuries to take their rest,
   A vast uncounted band.

And all who dwell on earth to-day,
Or young or old, will pass away,
Yet shall the ocean never stay
   From breaking on the shore,
Till the archangel's form shall stand,
One foot on sea and one on land,
And swear by God's almighty hand,
   That time shall be no more.

THE LIFE–LINE.

ALONG the coast of India
  A fearful typhoon raged,
And on the life of man and beast
  A deadly warfare waged.
Swift, terrible, destructive,
  With seeming murderous glee
It devastated villages
  And plunged into the sea.

There, on the helpless vessels
  Its fiercest fury fell,
Dismanteled ships, the sea engulfed,
  None left their fate to tell.
The waves in answering madness rose
  To meet the angry sky,
And thundered on the rocky coast
  Their billows mountain high.

The English frigate Enterprise,
  With more than four-score souls,
Was striving bravely with the gale,
  Amid the rocks and shoals,
To reach the shores of Andaman,
  Whose prison turrets gleamed
From out the blinding rack of storm,
  When baleful lightning streamed.

But vainly with the tempest, strove
   The staunchest ship, that day,
Dashed on the cruel, jagged rocks
   With force no power could stay.
The helpless sailors, all too soon,
   Were struggling with the waves,
And drowning, dying, one by one,
   They sank to watery graves.

On shore, some women convicts
   Were toiling up the beach,
Drenched with the rain-fall, as they strove
   Their prison home to reach.
They learned the dreadful peril,
   Above the tempest's breath
They heard the shriek of agony
   From those who strove with death.

They paused and turned, the awful sight
   A common purpose gave,
And pity woke in every breast
   A strong desire to save.
They struggled back from rock to rock,
   The nearest point to gain,
Made breathless by the whirling storm
   And black and blinding rain.

Hand clasped in hand, a line was formed,
   Which stretched from solid land,
To where the boiling billows' foam
   Tossed up the shifting sand.

The foremost, plunging boldly in,
  With hand-clasp firm and warm,
Drew from the seething cauldron forth,
  A helpless, human form.

Again and yet again she drew
  Man after man to land,
Impelled to strength and courage new
  By every clasping hand.
And when exhausted quite, at last
  She fell, as mortals will,
The next in line stepped bravely forth,
  Her sacred place to fill.

Of all that good ship's company,
  Not one had reached the land,
But for the saving power within
  A woman's helping hand.
Not one of all the women there,
  But had been overthrown
And buried by the furious waves,
  If she had stood alone.

*   *   *   *   *   *

Thus sisters, let us form the line,
  Each clasp another's hand,
And work to rescue sinking souls—
  An earnest, Christian band.
More dreadful than the angry sea
  Fanned by the typhoon's breath
Are the black waves of sin and crime,
  Which drag men down to death.

So happy in our homes of ease,
   We scarcely hear the cry
Of struggling souls temptation-tossed,
   Who fall and sink and die.
The clasping of a friendly hand,
   The help Christ came to give,
Would draw them to the sheltered shore,
   Where they might safely live.

Then in Christ's name united stand!
   Stand in His strength divine!
His tender, pitying love shall fill
   Each heart along the line.
His Spirit will endue with power,
   To rescue and to save
The souls, now lost and perishing,
   For whom Himself He gave.

As one by one the leaders fall,
   Supported by His grace,
The next in line shall forward move,
   And fill each vacant place.
Each consecrated life will win
   In Heaven its true renown,
Where every rescued soul shall shine,
   A jewel in love's crown.

THE SEA-SHELL.

HARK to the sea-shells' song!
A song so low and sweet,
It seems to but repeat
The whispered sigh
Of waves which die,
On beds of glistening sand,
Along the ocean strand.

Sometimes amid the notes,
I catch the tempest's breath,
Which tells of wreck and death,
The wailing cry
Of those who die,
And mid the angry waves,
Go down to unmarked graves.

Sometimes it seems to sing
Of all things strong and free,
Which dwell within the sea,
Where billows rise
To touch the skies,
And toss their snowy foam
Above the sea-shells' home.

Why do you sing, oh, shell!
Far from your native land,
Far from the wave-washed strand,

Where once you slept,
And faithful kept,
Through changing wind and tide
The treasures you would hide?

Do we not sometimes hear,
In our own souls a song,
Whose notes we would prolong,
A whispered chime,
Of that fair clime,
That land which hath no name,
The land from whence we came!

THE MIRAGE.

A DIM mist hung above the lake,
    The sky was dull and gray,
The passing breeze seemed scarce awake,
    To bear the barks away.

So noiselessly they stole afar,
    Like sheeted ghosts so pale,
The fog-wreaths twining every spar
    With shreds of misty veil.

The sun rose slowly from his bed
    Of amber tinted folds,
And silently his javelins sped
    Across the great lakes cold.

A sudden glory bathed the earth,
  A glory filled the sky,
As if a new world sprang from birth
  'Neath the All-seeing eye.

And swiftly on the low-hung clouds,
  A picture strangely fair,
The sea and ships with masts and shrouds
  Were painted on the air.

Then broader grew the wondrous scene,
  The canvas still unrolled,
Till hill and valley, clothed in green,
  And touched with morning's gold,

Swung lightly from the shining strand
  On cloud-banks dim and high,
While castle towers with turrets grand
  Rose dark against the sky.

An hour passed by, the breeze swept free,
  The sun shone in its strength,
And slowly faded ship and sea,
  And hill and tower, at length.

The blue sky arching over all,
  The wave-washed, rocky shore,
The distant hills and forests tall,
  The lake, sail-dotted o'er,

These still remained. The matchless view
  Spread grandly out on high,
And, touched with glory strange and new,
  Had vanished from the sky.

As fleeting as the joys of earth,
    As swift to pass away
As worldly pleasure is, whose birth
    Is followed by decay.

A faint, foreshadowing of bliss
    And glory of the skies,
Where heavenly joy eternal is,
    And beauty never dies.

TRUST.

TWO sisters by the casement white
    Looked on the sea one summer's night,
Its billows bathed in silver light.

A harvest moon and cloudless sky,
And great waves rising mountain high,
To toss their kisses to the sky.

They saw the shining path which lay
Like molten silver stretched away
Across the waters of the bay.

They saw the narrow line of sand
Between the ocean and the land,
The gray dunes farther up the strand.

The rocks which rear their massive forms,
Sole guardians of the coast in storms,
Through winter chills, or summer warms.

They saw the vessels come and go
Across the moonbeam's brightest glow,
As white-winged birds flit to and fro.

Then one said softly, " Oh, how fair!
On sea or land, in earth or air,
God's beauty shineth everywhere.

" But most of all beside the sea,
Whose ceaseless anthem seems to me
Fit symbol of eternity."

The other shivered as with pain,
And on her cheeks there came the stain
Of falling tears, like summer rain.

" The sea so cruel is," she said,
" Its terrors, like a mantle spread,
Enwrap my heart with fear and dread.

"And ever in its undertone
There comes to me the bitter moan
Of drowning sailors overthrown.

"The foam-capped waves which beat the strand,
Gleam ghostly, like the beckoning hand
Of those who perish far from land.

" I hear rich freighted vessels groan
Beneath their burdens, and alone
Go down, unnoticed and unknown.

"And huge sea monsters follow fast
The shipwreck and the stormy blast,
To aid the tyrant in his task.

" Death rides triumphant on the wave;
The sea becomes a mighty grave,
With none to pity, none to save."

" Nay," said the first, "but sweetly still,
" The sea His mandate must fulfill,
Who made it by His word and will.

"Death comes to all, on sea or land,
Though why we may not understand,
We trust a Father's guiding hand.

"Why sin and sorrow came to dwell
In human hearts, we can not tell,
But God His love hath proven well.

"On land or sea alike, we share
His tender and protecting care,
His mercy shineth everywhere."

THREE FISHERMEN.

THREE fishermen down by the sea
  Sat mending their nets one day,
They were browned by the wind and the sun,
  And all were wrinkled and grey.

The first said,—" I was a boy
  When my father's ship went down—
I remember well that fearful night;
  It was wrecked in sight of town.

" My mother watched it and wept,
  As she clasped her children three,
Then she reared her boys in an inland town,
  But all of them follow the sea."

The second sighed as he said,—
  " It is not so long ago
Since the boat went down off Newfoundland,
  Which carried my brave boy Joe.

" Yes, I was a skipper then,
  And the second mate was he,
I lost my heart with my ship and boy,
  But I can not leave the sea."

The third one shook his head
　　As he said, half bitterly,—
"The sea has buried my wife and child,
　　And it's good enough for me.

"For nigh on sixty-years
　　It has been a home to me,
And I want my final resting-place
　　In the bottom of the sea."

Then they watched the sea and sky
　　And the white gulls sailing low,
And said,—"We must mend our nets to-day,
　　To-morrow a-fishing we go."

RELIGIOUS POEMS.

GOD.

GOD reigneth in the heavens,
 His glorious dwelling place,
God filleth with his presence,
 The immensity of space.
No living, sentient being
 On earth or farthest star
From life's great Sun and Center
 Can hold himself afar.

And vainly man desireth
 By shade of starless night,
Or folds of rayless darkness,
 To shield him from God's sight.
In vain on wings of morning
 To distant worlds would fly,
Nor Heaven nor hell can hide him
 From God's all-seeing eye.

God, by His Holy Spirit,
 To every soul draws near,
By every heart acknowledged
 In throbs of love or fear.
The willing and obedient
 Behold His face with joy,
The wicked and rebellious,
 Through sins, which peace destroy.

We can not help but touch Him,
　　Hemmed in on every side,
His love and law surround us,
　　Creator, King and Guide.
How shall we meet and greet Him?
　　He comes at our desire
The sun of life and glory
　　Or "a consuming fire."

CHRIST'S BLESSING.

LONG years ago, amid the hills
　　Of Judea, and beside her rills,
Walked the great Teacher, wise and strong,
Revealing truth, reproving wrong.

Around Him came with willing feet,
The eager crowd, His voice to greet,
The rich and poor, the great and small,
His words of wisdom were for all.

And so, one day, amid the throng,
Moved by an impulse pure and strong,
Came many mothers, in whose arms
Were laughing babies, full of charms.

And others led by tiny hand,
The little feet which scarce could stand,
And to the Savior pressing near,
His words of blessing staid to hear.

But those who sat as learners there,
Reproved them with a zealous care,
The Master must not be annoyed,
His sermon in effect destroyed.

And thrust them rudely back, who came
Such benison of love to claim,
They could not understand that He
Could stoop to such humility.

" Forbid them not," the Savior cried,
(With somewhat of reproof implied),
"Suffer the children thus to come,
Of such my kingdom is and home.

And ye, if ye are not as they,
So humble, teachable alway,
Ye can not dwell within my heart,
Nor of My kingdom share a part."

Then tenderly with fond caress,
He stooped each little one to bless,
And left, on brows uplifted there,
The touch of holy hands, in prayer.

Like ocean waves, which ebb and flow,
Earth's generations come and go,
And still like music's sweetest notes,
Christ's blessing down the centuries floats.

Dear children do you know how rare
The gift your Savior bids you share,

How priceless is the love which waits,
To open for you Heaven's gates?

And mothers is there aught for you,
In the sweet lesson ever new,
Of those who brought their darlings there,
And asked a blessing with a prayer?

Still waits our gracious Lord, to own
His little ones wherever known,
And offers from the world's alarms,
The shelter of His loving arms.

And all may share His heavenly calm,
His words of sweetness dropping balm,
His peace, deep-flowing, day by day,
The world nor gives nor takes away.

Still, beggars at His palace gate,
From early morn till evening late,
We come and meet where'er we stand,
The welcome of His outstretched hand.

" Come in and sup with Me," He saith,
" Believe, oh! ye, of little faith,
Accept My freely offered love,
My grace shall all-sufficient prove."

DIVINE COMPASSION.

DISCOURAGED, sick at heart and sad,
   With faint and failing breath,
The fiery prophet of the Lord
Who fled from the avenger's sword,
   Laid down and prayed for death.

Short time before, on Carmels height,
   With faith which knew no fear,
He watched the heaven-descending fire,
Which answering came at his desire,
   To prove Jehovah near.

And filled with burning zeal for God,
   And courage stern but grand,
The false, blind leaders of the blind,
No pity in his heart could find
   Who fell beneath his hand.

But weak and wailing as a child,
   In darkness and despair,
Beneath the broom-tree's welcome shade
Elijah's weary head was laid,
   And death, his only prayer.

Then mid the silence and the calm
  Came slumber deep and sweet,
And lo! a voice said tenderly,
"The journey is too great for thee,
  Arise, arise and eat."

No message of reproach to bear,
  No stern reproof to give —
The gentle angel only brought
The sustenance the prophet sought,
  That he might eat and live.

A heaven-sent messenger of love,
  With sympathy to greet, —
A father's tender care to prove,
By strength and blessing from above,
  His human needs to meet.

Oh! tender pity of our God,
  The God in whom we trust,
He knoweth every child by name,
Considereth our feeble frame,
  Remembering it is dust.

He sends to comfort weary ones,
  And bid their sorrows cease —
With shelter from the burning sun
And sweet repose when toil is done, —
  The angel of his peace.

THE REVEALER.

IN the dim ages of the past,
   Earth's morning twilight hour,
Jehovah, God, revealed himself
   Through miracles of power:
The thundering of Sinai's mount
   Thrilled every heart with fear,
The cloudy pillar and the flame
   Proclaimed his presence near.

His own strong hand and mighty arm
   His chosen people led
Triumphant over vanquished foes
   And hosts of gory dead;
His faithless, wayward followers,
   Along their devious path,
His jutice and his greatness learned,
   Through scourgings of his wrath.

When in the fullness of the time,
   The great Revealer came
No fiery lightnings girt him round
   Nor panoply of flame,
The tender, loving heart of God,
   Shone through his holy face,
With wondrous words his lips proclaimed
   The gospel of free grace.

The miracles his hands preformed
 Appealed to human need,
The ruler of the wind and waves
 Could still the hungry feed;
Could heal the sick, restore the blind,
 The sinning could forgive,
Could cast out demons, raise the dead,
 And teach men how to live.

" Teach us to pray," disciples said,
 Who gathered 'round his knee,
" We can not reach the ear of God,
 We come to learn of Thee."
" Not with vain words," the Christ replied,
 " Which heathen love to use,
Nor tiresome round of lengthy prayers,
 The gift of heaven abuse;

" Nor clad in empty, outward forms,
 Shalt thou approach His throne,
Nor seeming unto men to fast,
 Shalt make thy wishes known;
' Our Father ' when thou prayest say,
 And He will hear thee call,
One is your Father, even God,
 And ye are brothers all."

MORE LABORERS.

"GO work to-day" the Master saith,
  "My vineyard waits for thee,
Broad is the field, the harvest white,
  From river unto sea!
The reapers still too few remain,
  They fall beside the way,
Worn with the labor, and the heat
  And burden of the day."

The weary cry of sin-sick souls,
  Throughout our broad, free land,
From North to South, with single voice
  Re-echoes this command:
The crowded cities of the East,
  Sin-darkened each and all,
The wide, green prairies of the West,
  Repeat the Master's call.

The heathan nations from afar,
  Stretch out their empty hands,
Uncounted millions worshiping
  Strange gods, in many lands;
The door is open, wind and tide
  Each sail shall kindly greet,
The ocean islands wait to hear
  The music of your feet.

They plead by all their human wants,
    By sins still unforgiven,
The right of every deathless soul
    To learn of God and heaven;
"Come, help us, for our need is great,
    Come while it is to-day,
Our time is short, this fleeting life
    Will soon have passed away."

Are there no idle hands which wait,
    For service for their Lord?
No willing and obedient hearts
    Who gladly hear his word?
No steadfast souls from doubts removed
    Whose feet perchance have trod
The thorny paths, by peril marked,
    Which reach the heights of God!

Have not these, with uplifted gaze,
    Beheld the Saviors face,
That they should willing servants be,
    To tell his matchless grace?
With sandaled feet, and shrinking not
    From sacrifice and loss,
Still up the steeps of Calvary,
    To bear the heavy cross.

Are there no hearts of joy bereft,
    Bowed down by sorrow's load,
Who in the balm of work, may find
    Strength for the lonely road?

Content if he, with thorn-crowned brow,
  Shall walk beside the way,
And on the spirits bleeding wounds,
  His hand of healing lay.

"Go, work, *To-day*," the Master saith,
  The hour of toil is brief,
In swift succession follow blade
  And grain and garnered sheaf:
And he who for his Lord has wrought,
  With talents *ten* or *one*,
Will in the hour of reckoning hear
  The gracious words, "Well done."

THE MESSENGER.

WAY-WORN and weary, with the grime
  And dust of travel-soil,
Heaped thickly by the hand of time
  And journey's lengthened toil;
Scorched with the heat of torrid lands,
  And parched with thirsting pain,
Wound slowly through the desert sands,
  The caravan's long train.

Day after day, the welcome word,
  The Arabs failed to bring,
Day after day, no voice they heard,
  To tell of cooling spring—

They saw the last sent forth, to spy
  The fountain's crystal brim,
Loom dark against the sunset sky,
  Far on the desert's rim.

But pausing suddenly, he stood
  A moment, as spell-bound,
In rapt and listening attitude,
  Held by some distant sound,
Then whirled and toward the jaded throng
  Rode through the twilight pale,
With the long gallop, swift and strong,
  Which told the welcome tale.

While ever and anon his voice,
  Like herald sent before
To bid their fainting hearts rejoice,
  The shout of "water" bore—
From far, his well-trained ear, had caught
  The talismanic word
By others sent, which thither brought,
  His soul with pleasure stirred.

Thus toiling through the sands of time
  With halting steps and slow,
As pilgrims in an alien clime,
  Earth's thirsting millions go.
Truth's precious fountain who shall win?
  The cooling streams are, where?
Whose waters quench the fires of sin,
  And slake the thirst of care.

Oh! watchful heralds, sent before,
   The healing springs to spy,
The hour grows late, and more and more
   Your brothers faint and die.
Ride swiftly, messengers of peace,
   Ring out your words of cheer!
Bear to each burdened heart release,
   "Salvation's fount is near."

FAITH, HOPE AND CHARITY.

FAITH is a firm, belief in all
   Which will be, or has been,
The inward evidence of that
   Which eye has never seen.
By faith we tread those holy heights,
   Where angels trembling stand.
Faith is the ladder by whose rounds
   We climb to God's right hand.

Hope is the anchor sure, which holds
   When storms assail life's bark,—
The guiding star which brightly gleams,
   When tempests gather dark.
It lights the straight and narrow way,
   Through earth's bewildering maze,
The valley and the shadow dim,
   Are glorious with its rays.

But better far than faith or hope,
   More Christ-like and more pure,
The heaven-born, holy charity,
   Which all things doth endure.
The humble love which envieth not,
   In patience suffering long,
Thinking no evil, hoping still,
   And meekly bearing wrong.

The brotherhood of man it binds
   In tenderest sympathy,
To every erring penitent,
   It brings a pardon free.
Redeemer, Mediator, Lord,
   With access to the throne,
And faith and hope to man are given,
   By God's great love alone.

THE REFUGE.

As the shadow of a great rock in a weary land."

WHAT though the noonday sun
    Beats fiercely o'er my head,
With'ring each perfumed flower
    Along the path I tread;
What though the breeze which fans,
    Be like the Simoon's breath,
That sweeps the desert sands,
    Swift harbinger of death;
Kept by God's changeless love,
    Led by His tender hand,
Within the shadow of the Rock
    Secure my feet shall stand.

What though the changing sky
    With clouds be overcast,
And joy's frail blossoms fly
    Before the stormy blast ;
And hopes which budded fair,
    In life's glad morning hour,
Lie blossomless and bare
    Beneath the tempest's power;
However wild the shock,
    Whatever ills betide,
Within the covert of the Rock,
    In safety I will hide.

What though above the hill
   The western sun shines low,
And night-winds, damp and chill,
   From frozen regions blow:
While singing birds have flown
   And flower and leaf are dead—
No pillow, save a stone,
   Remaineth for the head,
When Death, his fingers cold,
   Upon my lids hath pressed,
Within the shadow of the Rock
   In sweetest dreams I'll rest.

PEACE.

"MY PEACE I GIVE UNTO YOU."

'TIS said, amid the desert sands,
   A little way-side flower
Folds in its cup, a drop of dew,
Through all the noon-tide hour.

A tiny drop, by night distilled,
   Yet keeping fresh and sweet
The little plant, through all the glow
   Of noon's most fervid heat.

The sun may burn, the sands may parch
   Each green and living thing,
But still the little flower blooms on,
   Fed by its hidden spring.

At eve its leaves are opened wide,
　To catch the falling shower,
At dawn it folds its petals close,
　To guard the heaven sent dower.

And thus, along life's barren wastes
　By weary footsteps trod,
Is hidden in the Christian's heart
　The holy peace of God.

The sands beneath his feet may burn,
　The mid-day sun ride high,
And love's most cherished hopes and plans
　About him withered lie.

The fever of noon's hurrying stress,
　Through all his veins may flow,
The cup he quaffs, bear to his lips
　The bitter taste of woe;

But peace, deep hidden in his soul,
　From God's unfailing spring,
The freshness of perennial spring,
　About his years shall fling.

Oh! blessed gift of love divine,
　Within our heart of hearts,
We pray thee tarry evermore,
　Until life's day departs.

"NEVER YET HEARD."

"HAVE you heard of the doctrine of Jesus,
   Of Jesus who made the sick whole?"
Asked a Christen physician and teacher,
   Who sought to save body and soul:

"Have you heard of the doctrine of Jesus,
   Of One who is mighty to save?
Of the. God who alone can redeem us
   From sin, and from death and the grave?"

Then mournful and low was the answer,
   Whose whisper the pallid lips stirred,
But thrilling the heart of the teacher
   With pain— "I have never yet heard."

And softly stole one and another,
   That wonderful story to hear,
As told by the gentle physician
   In accents most tender and clear.

And ever the sorrowful answer,
   Her spirit to sympathy stirred,
One after another responded,
   "Ah! no, I have never yet heard."

The home was a home filled with beauty,
  For wealth and adornment were there,
Long corridors, stately and ornate,
  And courts full of flowers most rare.

And the daughter, a fair, fading blossom,
  Consumption had marked for his own,
Was loved with as tender affection,
  As human love ever has known.

But how hopeless and dark was the future,
  How full of misgiving and dread,
No light on the Valley of Shadows
  Their vain superstitions had shed.

And into that horror of darkness,
  Her spirit was drifting away,
With knowledge of only dumb idols,
  To whom in its anguish to pray.

Oh! Christians, whose earliest childhood
  Was bright with that story of love,
Is there nothing wherewith in lifes manhood
  Your love for the Master to prove?

No way, through your own lips or others,
  Thereby you may utter a word
In the ears of the perishing millions,
  Who never of Jesus have heard?

WHILE I SLEPT.

ONE day, in a wide, green meadow,
    A father and child sat down,
To rest, 'neath a great tree's shadow,
    Apart from the busy town.

The father was kind and tender,
    The daughter, a child of three,
Was lovely in form and feature,
    As fair as a child could be.

The birds in the boughs sang sweetly,
    And hushed was the drowsy air,
The father had left behind him
    His burden of work and care.

And while the little one prattled,
    And gathered the blossoms sweet,
(Great handfulls of snow-white daisies)
    And scattered them at his feet,

He slept, but his dreams were mingled
    With voices of child and bird,
With rustle of lightest footsteps,
    Or leaves by the soft wind stirred.

At length he awoke in terror,
  A silence which seemed to chill,
Had pierced through the folds of slumber
  And wakened his dormant will.

In haste and in fear he sought her,
  Loud calling in tenderest tones,
"Come hither, my little daughter,
  Oh! where has my dear one flown? "

But echoes alone gave answer,
  And nothing of sight or sound,
Betrayed where the missing darling
  Had wandered, and might be found.

At last, in a distant corner,
  Where sharply the bank fell down
To meet with the rapid river,
  Which hurried away to town,

He peered through the gathering shadows
  And saw on the rocks below,
A tangle of silken tresses,
  The gleam of a robe of snow.

He sprang down the bank, and folded
  The form in his fond embrace,
And covered with frenzied kisses
  The pallid but beautiful face.

In vain—love could not restore her,
   And ever his cry, as he wept,
"She perished, my darling, my daughter,
   She perished, while idly I slept."

Oh! Christians, who slumber serenely,
   At ease in your pulpit or pew,
Can it be, that such bitter repining,
   May come at the last unto you?

When the years of your dreaming are over,
   Will you waken in sorrow to weep?
Are friends going down to perdition,
   Are souls being lost, while you sleep?

PALMS.

FROM out Arabia's burning sands,
   The stately palm-trees rise,
Uplifting feathery fronds, to catch
   The brightness of the skies.
Low at their feet the quenchless springs,
   Of pure, sweet waters flow,
Affording strength and sustenance,
   Wherewith the palm-trees grow.

The winter's storms, the summer's heat,
   Unheeded pass their way,
The palm-trees spread their branches clothed
   In verdure day by day.

And generations come and go,
　And gather for their need
From luscious clusters drooping low,
　The fruit whereof they feed.

Thus he, whose life is hid with Christ,
　Shall like the palm-trees grow,
In stately beauty, reaching up,
　Where airs diviner glow.
By streams of living waters fed,
　On heavenly hills which rise,
The fountain is God's changeless love,
　Which nothing good denies.

Temptations beat with summer's heat,
　About his path at will,
The world's cold scorn, or rude rebuff,
　As vainly seek to chill.
Day after day, and year by year,
　The ripened fruit he bears,
Of holy living, kindly deeds,
　And christian love and prayers.

THE RISEN LORD.

IN the gray dawn of early morn
  They came, with willing feet,
The loving women with their load
  Of spices rich and sweet.
And mournfully and tenderly,
  Oppressed by doubt and gloom,
They spake of Him, the crucified,
  Who lay within the tomb.

His words of gracious sweetness, sure
  They never could forget,
Though on the lips which uttered them,
  The seal of death was set.
Love still would guard the cherished form
  From nature's swift decay;
But who from that sealed sepulcher
  Could roll the stone away?

Thus questioned they with troubled hearts,
  But neither grief nor fear
Their hastening steps delayed, and soon
  The new-made tomb was near—
Behold! in place of sentinel
  Rock-hewn and grim and bare,
An angel, with a smiling face
  And blessing, met them there.

How oft in duty's pathway still
   The great stone seems to lie:
"The way is hedged, we can not pass,"
   In bitterness we cry.
But pressing boldly toward the door
   We find it open stands,
While Joy and Blessing smiling wait
   And greet with outstretched hands.

The paths of Christian usefulness
   Are waiting willing feet,
The stone is rolled, the bolts and bars
   No longer hindering meet.
All lands are ready for the truth,
   Once far-off lands, are near,
The message of the risen Christ
   All nations wait to hear.

"Go, tell my people everywhere,
   I go before them still,
I lead, I dwell with those who strive
   To do my work and will."
The Lord is risen, Christian hearts,
   Awake, rejoice and sing!
Spread the glad tidings far and wide,
   And grateful tribute bring.

PRAYER.

HOW shall I seek for what my soul desires,
　　How ask for that which seemeth best to me?
With strong importunate pleading which aspires
　　To move the throne of Heaven on bended knee!
With faith which mountains can remove, and cast
　　Into the sea of difficulties passed?

Strange consciousness of power must rest on them
　　Who rising from long sickness, can attain
To touch of His celestial robe the hem,
　　And know no more of weariness or pain;
Who ask a blessing, and the answer see,
　　"According to thy faith be it to thee."

But all too weak my hands, too dim mine eyes,
　　Too short my sight, such swift response to see;
I know not if the thing I seek were wise,
　　If that which seems so fair were best for me;
I can not claim by right the fruit, whose wine
　　Might change to bitterness on lips of mine.

For they are many who have lived to bless
　　The hand which oft withheld the gift desired,
Whose prayers unanswered claim a larger stress
　　Of gratitude than things by prayer acquired.
Who asked unwittingly, and blindly sought,
　　What countless evils in its train had brought.

But this I know, dear Lord, thy loving hand
  All seeming ill can overrule for good,
Though leading through what seems a barren land
  Thy care will well supply the needed food;
And kept in perfect peace his soul shall be,
  Whose trust, in storm or calm, is stayed on thee.

This then my prayer, that Thou wilt grant each day
  The strength required its duties to fulfill,
And grace sufficient for whatever may
  My portion be, of earthly good or ill.
In joy or sorrow, with each rising sun
  To say, " Father, thy holy will be done."

GOD'S HOUSE.

" Howbeit the Most High dwelleth not in temples made with hands."

BY God's command, in ancient days,
  His people built, for prayer and praise,
A tabernacle they could bear
Along their journeying with care.
Wherein the table of his law
Might rest, and where with solemn awe,
His priests might daily enter in,
To offer sacrifice for sin.
And ever in the holiest place,
Where cherubim with smiling face,
Their golden wings out-stretched, to meet
Above the sacred mercy seat,

And where alone the high-priest knelt,
The symbols of Jehovah dwelt,
A visible and outward sign ⌐
Of presence holy and divine.
And when at length, that wandering band,
Of strangers in a desert land,
Had reached and won their place and home,
A mighty nation had become—
And kings, with wealth and wisdom crowned,
Upon their regal throne were found,
With Solomon in glad accord
They reared the temple of the Lord.
A splendid structure, which should stand,
A beacon light to all the land,
And to the heathen world proclaim,
"One God, Jehovah is his name."

If mortal man might build a place
For him, who fills all heavenly space,
If carven wood and gems and gold
In bonds the mighty God might hold,
No fairer palace need be sought,
Than skill of Soloman had wrought.
With treasures gathered from afar,
With wealth of peace and spoil of war,
With gold of Ophir deftly won,
And cedars tall of Lebanon,
And cunning workman sought with care
The holy temple to prepare—
In silence rose the walls of stone,
Each fitted to its place alone;

No sound of hammer there was heard,
Nor blow of axe the zephyr stirred,
But beam on beam with matchless skill
Rose, its appointed place to fill,
And door and floor and column tall,
And oracle, and carved wall,
Were overlaid with lavish hand
In gold, by Solomon's command.
With patient skill the workmen wrought,
And when to full completion brought,
And while the gathered nation poured
Their sacrifice, before the Lord,
The glory of his presence came
To overshadow like a flame,
The temple honored by his name.

Doth he, who filleth with his grace,
The vast immensity of space,
Who formed the earth, and spread on high
The azure canopy of sky,
With worlds on worlds, and lit in turn,
The dazzling suns which blaze and burn,
Doth He require through human care,
An earthly dwelling-place to share?
Enthroned in majesty above,
Encompassed by eternal love,
He hath no need than man should bring
To him the humble offering,
Of gilded wall or chiselled stone,
Who hath the universe his own.

But we, the creatures of his grace
Subjected still to time and place,
We gather by love's common law,
That haply we may nearer draw,
And wings of faith and prayer employ,
To reach the primal source of joy.
And thus along the centuries stand
The gray catherdrals, vast and grand,
Which wise men, in religious mood,
Built for their own and others good.
And thus throughout our own, broad land,
From east to west, on either hand,
We mark unnumbered spires arise,
Like fingers pointing to the skies,
Which tell where congregations meet
And worship at the Master's feet.

The weary traveler sore distressed,
By cold and hunger long oppressed,
The wayside inn with pleasure views,
Where food and rest his strength renews,
And through the helpful comfort lent,
Pursues his journey well content.
Thus to the strongest of our race,
Come with a touch of saving grace,
The rest and strength along the road,
We gather at the house of God,
By his own Spirit comforted
And by his heavenly manna fed.
Now, as of old, he waits to greet
His children at the mercy seat,

And manifests his Spirit, where
Receptive souls await in prayer,
While those who gather in his name,
His promised presence there, may claim.
And thus through means we well may prize,
The church invisible doth rise,
A tower of strength, and broader grown
Than narrow walls of wood and stone,
Embracing in its power to bless,
All forms of human wretchedness,
The church, which founded on Christ's Word,
Shall ever stand, its God the Lord.

"PEACE ON EARTH."

THIS was the song which the angels sang—
    Over the Judean hills it rang,
  Telling the tale of Christ's birth,
To nations and people who hearken still—
" Glory to God, and God's good will,
  Peace, his peace upon earth."

This is the message the years unfold,
Made clearer now, than in days of old,
  When it fell on the shepherd's ears.
Like a falling star from its heavenly height,
Strange in its sweetness and robed in light,
  But filling their hearts with fears.

This is the secret which Christmas tells,
Sweet as the silvery chime of its bells,
  Over and over again,
Set to the music of kindly deeds,
Which clothes the naked, the hungry feeds,
  " Peace and good will to men. "

Love in its holy unselfishness,
  Giving its own, some other to bless,
  This is the Christly love,
That wakes in the heart of humanity still,
Blessing and joy, and peace and good-will,
  Which the angels sing above.

THE PLACE OF REST.

OH! land of rest,
      Beyond the toiling and the tears,
Beyond the doubting and the fears,
      And joy repressed,
Which dim the beauty of this life,
And make us feel amid its strife,
      That death is best.

      We know not where
Thy peaceful valleys stretch away,
Bright with the light of endless day,
      And skies so fair,

Where life's pure stream forever flows,
And fadeless blooms love's thornless rose,
    Whose sweets we share.

    We can not know
What work our hands may find to do,
Where all are good and pure and true,
    No want nor woe,
No more of weariness or pain,
No grief to mar or sin to stain,
    Nor tears to flow.

    But this is best,
Our Savior will the place prepare,
For all who His salvation share,
    (Are we so blest) ?
And there by His abounding grace,
We each shall find a fitting place,
    And be at rest.

THE HEALING TOUCH.

AMID the eager multitude
    Who followed, close to press
And catch the wondrous words of Him
    Who came to heal and bless,
Was one, so weak and ill her frame,
She scarcely dared his notice claim.

Though thrust aside, and jostled oft,
    By those who backward held,
Still nearer to his side she stole,
    By her great need impelled;
"If I but touch His garment's braid,
I shall be healed and blessed," she said.

A moment, and the seamless robe,
    By passing breezes fanned—
To which her humble faith had clung—
    Was wafted to her hand.
A single touch, as on He sped,
And all her pain and illness fled.

Dear Lord, whose love is manifest,
    In every way of Thine,
Here still are sin-sick souls, who wait
    The healing touch divine.
Walk Thou our streets, and let us hear
The rustling of Thy garments near.

The cares of life surround and crowd—
  Thy shining face to hide—
And doubts and fears a conflict wage
  To keep these from Thy side.
Come Thou, with saving power, to them,
Though they but touch Thy garment's hem.

THE FIELD.

" AMONG so many, what are they,
    Five loaves, two fishes small,
Send thou the multitude away
  We can not feed them all! "
Thus reasoned they, who once had seen
  Displayed, the power divine,
Which at the Cana marriage feast
  Changed water into wine.

We think of earth's uncounted hosts
  Who never heard the name
Of Him, who left His throne of light,
  And as their Savior came!
We shrink appalled before the thought,
  "And who are we," we cry,
" So few to bear the bread of life
  To those who faint and die! "

But He, who in that desert place
  His banquet freely spread,
And fed the hungry thousands there,
  Is not He still our head?
"Go ye in all the world," He saith,
  "And everywhere proclaim
(Where still earth's teeming millions wait)
  This gospel in My name."

TRUTH.

SCATTER the seeds of truth,
  Beside all waters sow,
The germs wait in immortal youth
  God's time wherein to grow.
Fear not! though the long night
  Its shadows o'er them cast,
A thousand years are in God's sight
  As yesterday, when passed.

Not every one who sows,
  Perchance with tears and pain,
The blessed privilege e'er knows
  Of gathering in the grain.
It may be thine to till,
  Another's hand to reap,
But duty's record, faithful still,
  Eternal love shall keep.

Think not truth disappears
    Within the age's tomb,
The aloe sleeps a hundred years,
    Then bursts in sudden bloom;
And time, the handmaid fair,
    Brings round the perfect hour,
While labor doth the soul prepare,
    To wake the century's flower.

Truth, like a river deep,
    Fed by unnumbered rills,
Where hidden springs in silence keep,
    Eternal as the hills,
Its own deep channel wears,
    Still broadening toward the sea,
And life within its bosom bears
    On to eternity.

Truth shall all barriers break,
    And whether late or soon,
With the strong flow of tides which make
    Beneath the harvest moon,
Shall flood the world with light—
    A never-setting sun;
While error hides in darkest night,
    For God and truth are one.

THE TRIED STONE.

"Behold, I lay in Zion a chief corner stone."

STONE upon stone, the granite pile
   Uprose in massive strength,
A work of art, which seemed to bring
   Completion near at length.

With nicest care each carven block
   Allotted space to fill,
Was chiselled by a master's hand,
   Obeyed a master's will.

When suddenly, from dome to base
   A shiver seemed to run,
The patient work of weary months
   A moment had undone.

The corner stone imperfect proved,
   A flaw so slight, the care
Of skillful workmen's practiced eyes,
   Had scarce perceived it there.

But tested by that crushing weight
   It yielded, marred and bent—
And lo! a seam from base to dome
   The splendid structure rent.

But not like this, thene corr stone
  Of old in Zion laid,
Whereon to build the church of God,
  With majesty arrayed.

Rejected by the builders oft,
  By men, despised, betrayed,
Jesus, the well belovéd son,
  The corner stone was made.

Tried in temptation's fiercest fires,
  Ambition, avarice, fame,
The glittering pomp of wealth and power,
  With pleading voices came.

In music sweet to human ears,
  He heard the children sing—
Casting their garments at his feet—
  " Hosanna to the King."

By bitter persecution tried,
  Hatred and malice sped
To pour the vials of their wrath
  On his devoted head.

The heavy cross, the open shame,
  The death of torture slow,
The burden of a great world's guilt,
  A great world's weight of woe.

By friends deserted and denied,
  By foes without; within,
In all points tempted, tested, tried,
  But ever without sin.

Build wide, build high the Christian church
  Upon this corner stone,
A tower of strength its walls will prove,
  And God will bless his own.

WHAT OF THE NIGHT?

"WATCHMAN, from thy lofty tower
      Peering through earth's gloomy night,
Tell us, at the present hour
  Can'st thou see the morning's light ?
Are the mountain tops sun-kissed,
  Hath the dawn unbarred her way,
Skies of pink and amethyst,
  Ushering in the golden day ?"

"Yes," the watchman's voice replies,
  "Though the night of sin is long,
There is promise in the skies,
  Hope for man, for God is strong,
And His spirit rests with power
  On His people; while they pray
Falls the pentacostal shower
  Full of blessing on their way."

Not alone, the watchman dwells,
  Shut his guarded tower within;
But a mighty army swells,
  Beating back the hosts of sin,

Lifting up the standard high
  In His name on whom they call;
Hear ye not the battle-cry?
  "God and Christ shall conquer all!"

In the promises is light,
  God, the mighty God, shall give
Strength and victory, to the right,
  And His truth forever live.
Down the ages floats His voice,
  Father, Comforter, and Friend,
Pledged in one, work on, rejoice,
  "I am with you to the end."

THE ANSWER.

"Ask and ye shall receive."

A FRAIL and helpless crippled child
    Lay on her little bed
And sighed: "How worthless is my life,
  'T'were better I were dead!
My feet can on no errands run,
  My hands no service give,
My voice, alas! is but a moan,
  And wherefore should I live?"

Thus to her friend and pastor spake
  The little girl one day,
Who answered: "There is power in prayer,
  Dear child, and you can pray."

The seed, wind-wafted by his words,
  Sprang up within her soul,
And thenceforth from her bed of pain
  Her prayers like incense stole.

A little while, and all around,
  Sweet showers of blessing came,
And dumb lips spake, and hearts were touched
  By Pentacostal flame;
And souls from darkness into light
  By hands unseen were led,
Three-score, into God's kingdom born,
  Who erst in sin were dead.

Then to the crippled child release
  By God's command was given,
The pain-racked frame no longer held
  The spirit ripe for Heaven.
And 'neath her pillowed head was found
  A slip of paper laid,
With sixty names inscribed thereon,
  The souls for whom she prayed.

Her life was brief, a little span,
  The end a glad release,
For sorrows compassed her about,
  And only death brought peace.
But on the crown prepared for her—
  A diadem complete—
These names were set, as stars to shine
  And laid at Jesus' feet.

WILLING SERVICE.

" GO build me a house," said the Master,
   " A place where my name shall be known,
A beautiful tent for my worship,
   The pattern to you shall be shown,
Go, gather the gold and the jewels,
   Which all the true-hearted shall bear
And build up a place for mine altars,
   My presence shall dwell with you there."

Then Moses returned to the people,
   And gave them the message he brought,
And swiftly was heaped at his bidding
   The gold and the silver he sought.
They cheerfully poured out their treasures,
   All eager the work to begin,
While the blue and the purple, fine linen,
   The wise-hearted women did spin.

They proffered their bracelets and earrings,
   Those free-hearted women of old,
And brought their most precious of jewels,
   Their rings and their fillets of gold.
And soon rose the Lord's sanctuary.
   All fair was the dwelling within,
With curtains of goat's hair and linen,
   The wise-hearted women did spin.

So stirred were the hearts of the people,
　　So freely they brought of their store,
The leaders were forced to restrain them,
　　For building they needed no more.
The cloud and the flame hovered over,
　　In token of work nobly done,
The glory of God was enfolded
　　In curtains the women had spun.

Like them, let us bring to God's service,
　　Oh! wise-hearted women, to-day,
Whatever of gold or of silver,
　　Of love or of labor we may,
'Till His temples are everywhere builded,
　　His banner in all lands unfurled,
And Christ with his people abiding,
　　His glory shall fill the whole world.

CHRIST AT THE WELL.

TO Jacob's ancient fountain,
　　With waters deep and still,
The woman of Samaria
　　Her bucket brought, to fill.
And 'mid the gathering shadows
　　Beheld a stranger there,
Who waited, worn and weary,
　　The cooling draught to share.

And as she gave, he told her
  Of things so strangely true,
Her troubled conscience pained her
  For secrets which he knew.
He told her of that Fountain
  Whence healing waters flow,
And whosoever drinketh
  Thereof, no thirst shall know.

And still, along life's pathway,
  On mountain top, or dell,
Where e'er we draw for water,
  Christ sits beside the well.
One drinks of worldly pleasure,
  But hears his gentle voice,
" There is a joy unmeasured
  Thy spirit to rejoice."

One bows before ambition,
  And clasps the flowing bowl
Whose fiery waters shrivel,
  And dwarf the human soul.
Then speaks the voice of Jesus,
  " Drink of the draught I bring,
Ye shall be sons and daughters,
  Of the eternal King."

One thinks with earthly riches
  His soul to satisfy,
And gathers gold and jewels
  A measureless supply—

Christ says: "In earthly garners
   The moth and rust decay,
But here is heavenly treasure,
   Which fadeth not away."

And one, by love's sweet fountain,
   Drinks of its waters pure,
And dreams of joys unchanging,
   Which shall through time endure—
But sees through blinding tear-drops,
   His cherished ones depart,
And Jesus softly whispers,
   "Son, give to me thine heart."

And one, by sorrow chastened,
   The bitter cup has quaffed,
And wounded, weak, and fainting,
   Made helpless by the draught—
Feels like a benediction,
   The touch of hand divine,
And hears the tone of pity,
   "Thy sorrows all are mine."

And one, by death's cold waters,
   That last, sad cup must drink,
Though heart within him faileth
   And flesh in terror shrink,
"I give thee life eternal,"
   The voice of Jesus cries,
"I give thee bliss supernal,
   A home beyond the skies."

LOOK AND LIVE.

STUNG by the serpent's fiery fangs,
　　Along the lonely plain,
The murmuring and rebellious hosts
　　Of Israel were slain.
Awe-struck and trembling, while their dead
　　In heaps about them lay,
The living and repentant thronged
　　At Moses' feet to pray.

" Help us, pray for us, we have sinned,"
　　Rang out their pleading cry;
" Beseech the Lord to pity us,
　　Ere all thy people die."
Then bowed the leader with his host
　　Before the mighty God,
And prayer for Israel lifted up,
　　" Remove Thy chastening rod."

He heard who veiled from them His face
　　By pillared cloud and flame,
And from His heavenly dwelling place
　　The gracious answer came:
" The God of all is merciful,
　　He will their sin forgive;
Lift high the brazen-serpent up,
　　And all who look shall live."

Still through the plains of discontent
    There throngs a weary band,
And Edom must be compassed ere
    They reach the promised land.
Sin's fiery serpents round them hiss,
    With venomed, deadly sting,
And only Christ, the crucified,
    Can their deliverance bring.

They wait the healing of His grace,
    Forgiveness through His name;
They wait for the uplifted cross,
    Salvation to proclaim.
'Tis ours, the blessed truths of God
    This dying world to give;
'Tis ours, to lift Christ's standard high,
    That all may look and live.

AWAKENING.

FROM sleep the brown earth springs,
    And robed in garments new
  With lips all wet with dew
The rapturous song of life re-sings.

Her myriad tongues upraise,
    In roseate flush of dawn
  And flower-besprinkled lawn,
The voiceless orisons of praise.

From sea to farthest shore,
    Through glossy-feathered throats,
  Their liquid mellow notes,
Her choir of singing-birds outpour.

To fringe and flower her trees,
    Her vast alembic fills,
  And incense sweet distils,
Borne Heavenward on each passing breeze.

When altar-fires are red,
    And praise from earth's cold sod,
  Ascends to nature's God,
Shall human hearts alone be dead?

Thou Fount of life supreme,
    Whence earth and air are thrilled
  And worlds uncounted filled,
Awake us from our winter's dream.

SUSTAINING GRACE.

"I bare you on eagle's wings."

FROM mountain eyrie bold and high,
 The half-fledged eaglet flies,
Content his new-found wings to try
 And soar to sunnier skies:
A moment hovers tremblingly,
 On wide wings tipped with snow,
O'er beetling crag and jagged rock
 And yawning gulf below,
Then with swift pinions cuts the air,
 And turns his undimmed eye
To fields of sunny ether, where
 His eagle brothers fly.

But wearied soon, the young wings droop,
 Unused such weight to bear,
The tired bird sinks, and soon must fall
 Save for the mother's care,
On strong, swift wings she hovers near,
 With loving, watchful eye,
She glides beneath the sinking form
 And bears it safe on high.
On eagle's wings, in truth, he soars,
 The tireless, grand and free,
Which safely bear him to his home,
 By craggy cliff or sea.

So pityingly, so tenderly,
  The loving Father's hand
Brought forth His ancient people, from
  The dark Egyptian land.
Their faith upheld by mighty signs
  And wonders all the way,
The cloudy pillar and the fire,
  To guide by night and day.
O'er trackless desert wastes, and through
  The deep, engulfing sea,
By manna fed, to Canaan led
  A nation strong and free.

And thus, Oh! fainting, trembling soul,
  His grace shall thee sustain,
And lead thee to His promised land;
  Perchance through paths of pain,
Or seas of trouble deep and wide,
  Or barren wastes of toil,
Or parched and murmuring by the way,
  While sins thy goods despoil;
Turned back, by giant doubts and fears,
  Which throng the border land,
And shrinking from the Jordan cold,
  Whose waves still wash its strand.

But patiently He bears with thee,
  Thy devious journey through,
The manna of His changeless love
  Falls on thy path like dew,
Thy guide in darkness as in day,
  His Christ once crucified,

The pillar and the flame shall be,
  Forever by thy side,
His grace like eagle's wings shall bear
  When dangers threaten thee,
And bring thee to Himself at last,
  A soul redeemed and free.

THE LORD'S.

THE silver and gold, are mine, saith the Lord,
  The cattle upon a thousand hills,
Deep down in the earth my gems are stored,
  My pastures are green beside the rills.

My sunshine warms, and my cool breeze fans,
  The fields of grain, where the soft dews fall,
And showers of blessing drop from My hands,
  For the earth is Mine and its fullness all.

And men are My stewards, they hoe and till,
  They gather in garners from field and vine,
And barter their merchandise at will,
  But they, and the treasures they heap, are mine.

WHAT IS IT, IN THY HAND?

A LONE, before the Holy One,
        And trembling,   Moses stood,
"How is it, I, a sinful man,
    Can work this wondrous good ?
The people will not hear my voice
    Nor listen when I speak;
For I am slow of utterance,
    And sinful, Lord, and weak."

Before him in its brightness burned
    The unconsuming flame,
The glory of the Lord of Hosts,
    From whence the answer came—
"But thou shalt lead my people forth,
    Jehovah gives command,
And surely I will go with thee,
    What is it in thine hand?"

So Moses answered, "But a rod."
    "Then cast it to the ground,"
And lo! a gliding serpent form
    In place of it was found.
"Put forth thy hand, and take again,
    That thou mayest know this hour,
The God who giveth work to thee,
    Endoweth thee with power."

Take courage, Christian hearts, to-day,
  For evermore the same,
Is He who led forth Israel's hosts,
  Jehovah is his name.
Still with the people of his love
  He walks with shining face,
And to the humblest follower,
  He gives the needed grace.

" What is it in thy hand ? "   He saith;
  Though but a shepherd's rod,
An instrument of power t'will prove
  In service for thy God.
Be swift to use, be strong and glad
  The needed toil to bear;
For victory is with the Lord,
  And all his people share.

Some humble instrument of toil,
  Some wealth at thy command,
Some gift to teach, some song to sing,
  What is it in thy hand ?
Bring to His storehouse all the tithes,
  In humble faith and love,
And consecrated service there,
  God's blessing soon shall prove.

ABIDE WITH ME.

" Abide with us for the day waneth. "

ABIDE with me, oh! Christ, amid lifes conflicts,
　　Its days of toil, and nights of weariness,
Amid the hurry of its ceaseless striving,
　　Abide with me to bless.

Abide with me, in every hour of trial—
　　My lips must press the bitter cup of pain,
By anguish wrung, the tears of human weakness,
　　My pillow oft will stain.

Abide with me, in hours of deepest sorrow,
　　My loved are passing, one by one, before
The young and fair, the strong and true, still hasten
　　On, to the other shore.

Abide with me, my day of life is waning,
　　The years are few, between me and the grave,
Soon I shall meet the Future, vast, eternal,
　　And Thou alone canst save.

Abide with me, in that dread hour of terror,
　　When soul and body sundered are, for aye,
Abide with me and guide my helpless spirit.
　　To realms beyond the sky.

Abide with me, oh! blessed Christ, when trembling
　Before the Judge of all the earth, I stand,
When I wouid sink beneath sin's dreadful burden,
　Uphold me by thy hand.

And wheresoe'er my place, by him appointed,
　To spend a long eternity shall be,
I know a Heaven of happiness awaits me '
　If Thou abide with me.

MEMORIAL POEMS.

THE THREE FRIENDS.

THREE maidens sat in the sunset glow,
 As friend with friend would meet;
And talked together in accents low—
And one was pale as the lily's snow,
And one had cheeks like the rose's blow,
 And all were fair and sweet.

From childhood's dawn to its closing day,
 Their lives, like a pleasant rill,
Had rippled along the selfsame way,
They had shared each other's books and play,
And whether merry, or sad, or gay,
 They had loved each other still.

But now before them lay paths untried,
 Awaiting their willing feet—
The hills would the narrow streams divide,
The rills become rivers, deep and wide,
To hurry on with a swollen tide,
 In the ocean depths to meet.

" I go" said one! "as a happy bride,
 In my loved one's home to dwell,
He has chosen me from the world beside,
And whatever of joy or woe betide,
I shall safely walk by a strong man's side,
 And carry my burdens well."

Then said another " I thirst to drink,
   From the waters pure and sweet,
Of knowledge—lesser aims must sink,
The way is steep, but I shall not shrink,
I will climb to the crystal fountain's brink,
   E'er I rest my weary feet.

"And when from the fount my cup I bear,
   With the dews distilled above,
I will pour for others a generous share,
And brighten the ways, so filled with care,
For this has been, and is still my prayer;
   Not yet is the time for love."

And the third one said, "I know not yet
   What the future bears for me,
But a pleasant home I can ne'er forget—
And to me it seems, like a jewel set
In a golden band where gems have met,
   A woman's best life must be."

They met no more in that sunset bower;
   When a few brief months had flown,
The fair, young bride, with her regal dower
Of health, and beauty, and wealth and power
Was stricken down in a single hour,
   And the strong man wept alone.

And the scholar lay on a bed of pain,
   As the weary weeks went by,
And heard from above, the sweet refrain,

"Come hither, earth's loss is heavenly gain,
Thy wish and thy prayer were not in vain,
    For the crystal fount is nigh."

The third one found in the path she trod,
    The friend whom her heart would wed,
And true to her duty and home and God,
Prepared to go—but the valley's clod,
And a narrow chamber beneath the sod,
    Were made for her bridal bed.

The arrow its mission must fulfill,
    And the archer's hand obey,
The shaft was sent by a Father's will—
And robed in her bridal beauty, still
And white, as a winter frozen rill,
    She slept on her wedding day.

The three had passed through the gates ajar,
    And entered the promised land.
Beyond the sun and the farthest star,
Through a pathway of light, o'er the hills afar,
In the home where the many mansions are,
    They met with a clasping hand.

The life, so brief to our mortal sight,
    Ere quenched in the darkness of tears,
With songs of the ransomed, in glory bright,
And harps and palms and garments of white,
Flows freely on, like a river of light,
    In the peace of unending years.

ASLEEP.

FOLD the tired hands on his breast,
　　Leave him to his dreamless rest;
Night, with dark and solemn brow,
Hides him in her chamber now,
And while years their numbers tell,
He shall slumber deep and well. •

Mourn not o'er the narrow bed,
Soft it pilloweth his head,
Earth's rude storms above him beat,
Howls the tempest at his feet:
Yet they wake no fever now,
Quickened pulse nor throbbing brow.

Chisel out the stone with care,
Plant the roses thickly there,
Thornless roses, bid them bloom
Sweetly, on the Christian's tomb,
Freed from sorrow sin and pain,
He shall waken yet again.

Waken? Nay he doth not sleep,
Wherefore o'er the low mound weep,
There the burden which he bore,
There the cast-off robe he wore,
He has reached life's highest goal,
Death could never bind the soul.

There the empty cage alone,
Whence the singing bird has flown,
Soaring to that land of light,
Where the worthy walk in white;
Where no notes of sorrow ring,
With the song the ransomed sing.

He has crossed the narrow street,
Where the seen and unseen meet,
Pain, and sin, and want, and woe,
Wailing through life's plaint below,
Peace and triumph, joy and love,
Pealing through life's song above.

Nevermore for him death's pain,
Nevermore earth's sin and stain,
Robed anew in garments pure,
Which forever shall endure:
Let the empty casket lie,
God has set the gem on high.

OUR BABY BOY.

THROUGH long, bright months, our home
    he filled
With beauty and with joy,
A gift, for which, we oft thanked God,
    Our winsome baby boy

Broad grew his noble brow, and white,
    More plump his rounded arms,
And every hour, but woke anew,
    Some added infant charms.

Thus passed his young life joyously,
    And months were but a name,
While summer regally went by,
    And gorgeous Autum came.

But sudden sickness paled his cheeks,
    With one declining day,
And laid him quiet in my arms,
    Who erst had been at play.

Through the dim watches of the night,
    I held him to my heart,
Dumb with a vague but shrinking dread,
    A fear that we must part.

Morn rose, and through the glowing East,
  The trooping colors came,
Lighting the dim arch of the sky,
  With hues of living flame.

But paler grew my baby's brow,
  More ghastly white his cheek,
And heavier lay upon my heart
  The thought I could not speak.

Vain the wild prayers, we breathed to Heaven,
  And tears which fell like rain,
God was too good to grant our child
  Earth's heritage of pain.

Yet watched we every lingering sign,
  And hung upon each breath,
Striving to fan life's flickering flame,
  And baffle even death.

But breathings of immortal life,
  His spirit's wings had stirred,
And long before the sun had set,
  The angel's song he heard.

Have pity on our weakness Thou,
  Once crucified and crowned;
Grant that our darling, lost on earth,
  In heaven may yet be found,

MAY 30TH.

REVERENTLY, tenderly, scatter the flowers,
   Beauty should honor the brave—
Earth like a mother, her mantle of green,
Folds o'er the breast of each sleeper serene,
Daisies have bloomed o'er these brothers of ours
   Since they were laid in the grave.

Patiently, lovingly, year after year,
   Hallow the turf o'er them pressed;
Storms in their fury above them have beat,
Winter has heaped his white snows at their feet,
Let the glad spring of refreshing appear,
   To brighten the place of their rest.

Gratefully, tearfully tell how they wrought,
   Speak of the goal they have won—
Worthy is he of the chaplet and crown
Who for another his life hath lain down—
Ours is the recompense victory brought,
   Peace when the battle was done.

Solemnly, earnestly, over them plight
   Fealty to country anew,
Nearer and dearer to manhood and youth
Make the old virtues of honor and truth,
Crown him the hero, who dares to do right,
   Dares to be faithful and true.

Silently, certainly, thus shall the hour
    Lessons of duty impart,
Peace hath her triumphs still hard to attain,
  Brief is the respite from traffic and gain—
Sorrow and love with beneficent power,
    Wait for each reverent heart.

HIS WILL.

"COME back, come back" we cry,
    "Oh! thou beloved return,"
Stretching out pleading hands,
  Dropping the tears which burn.
There comes no answer, save
  The voice so small and still,
"Be hushed, rebellious heart,
  It is thy Father's will."

"Come back, the years are long.
  Our hearts have weary grown,
Waiting thy loving smile,
  Missing thy tender tone."
No answer from the void—
  Dumb is death's mystery,
Save the eternal word,
  "Thy Father pitieth thee."

"Come back, our souls are tossed,
  On sorrow's stormy sea,
No harbor can we reach,
  Beloved, apart from thee;

Is thy bark moored amid
    The islands of the blessed?"
No answer save the cry,
    "But I will give thee rest."

"My thoughts are not thy thoughts,
    My ways are not thy ways,"
Saith the unchanging God,
    The one Ancient of days—
"High as the heavens above,
    Far as is East from West,
So are my thoughts removed,
    From those by thee possessed.

"But one thing thou dost know,
    I gave my Son, to be
Thy Savior, shall I then
    Withhold aught good from thee?
Thou canst not understand,
    The way is dark, but still
Thou canst believe and trust,
    It is thy Father's will."

LUA.

IN the full bloom of gracious womanhood,
  Loving and loved of all,
From home of luxury and light,
  She passed beyond recall.

A tender, faithful wife, a mother fond,
  A friend forever kind,
Her sweet, unselfish, woman's heart,
  Some good in all could find.

With clear conceptions of the truth, the right,
  She spurned the false, the wrong,
And builded all her daily life
  With beauty and with song.

A silent angel gently led her where
  God's splendor fills all space,
Through Heaven's unending years to share
  The glory of His face.

WHEREFORE ?

FOLD the hands so thin and small,
　　Lightly o'er the pulseless breast,
Though your tears as rain shall fall,
　　They will not disturb her rest—
Though her children round her stand,
　　Calling "Mamma" o'er and o'er,
E'en at touch of baby's hand
　　She will waken nevermore.

Wherefore, standing as she stood,
　　Center of a home, till now,
With the crown of motherhood
　　Resting on her saintly brow;
Wherefore was she called so soon,
　　Called to lay aside her crown,
Ere life's sun had reached high noon,
　　Care and comfort to lay down.

Though we question, though we call,
　　From the void comes no reply,
Death and silence over all,
　　Heedless of our bitter cry;
Silence, though the voice of love,
　　From the ages gone before,
With a sound all sounds above
　　Thunder at the sealed door.

Yet we know, a hand unknown
  Led her all the thorny way,
And a face beside her shone,
  Through the darkness as the day,
Filling all her soul with light,
  While the path of pain she trod,
Guiding through death's gloomy night,
  To the paradise of God.

Shall we question; shall we doubt
  Love unmeasured led the way ?
Never midnight yet without
  Morn behind it waiting lay.
Let the blessing of God's peace,
  Bid the stormy sea, "be still,"
Sorrow's sad complaining cease,
  At the fiat of His will.

ASSURANCE.

"If a man die shall he live again?"

WHERE hast thou flown, oh! friend
      of mine?
My soul goes forth, in search of thine,
  In search o'er land and sea;
From far off hills of glory bright,
  Through spaces filled with heavenly light,
  Canst thou not come to me?

A single word, a touch, a sign,
The clasping of that hand of thine,
　　One moment as of yore,
To show me thou dost not forget,
To tell me that thou lovest yet,
　　And I will ask no more.

I would not have thee linger here,
But show me that thou livest, dear,
　　That death no triumph knew,
Beyond the frail and crumbling clay,
Blown by his icy breath away,
　　Like drops of morning dew.

Through trackless space I fain would fly,
With yearning strong and bitter cry,
　　The cry of soul for soul—
Bereft and desolate, alone,
Where'er through darkness thou hast flown,
　　To reach thy heavenly goal.

Turn back a moment on thy way,
And give to-night one glimpse of day,
　　Assurance so divine;
The life which death could not destroy,
Thy free, glad life shall touch with joy,
　　And thrill this heart of mine.

Nay, must the dead return, to tell
The secrets death has guarded well,
　　Doth not our Lord declare

That, "where I am, my own shall be,
And there forevermore with me,
　My glory they shall share?"

Enough, I need not clasp thy hand,
Since thou art with the angel band,
　Nor could I hear thee call,
For deaf and dumb and blind am I,
To sign or language of the sky,
　But Christ reveals it all.

AMONG THE FLOWERS.

THEY heaped the blossoms above her grave,
　The grave of our beautiful dead.
Pale, creamy roses, and spotless pinks,
　Together their perfumes shed.
And the lily-bells and forget-me-nots
　Were blent with a tender grace,
And the pansies peered from amid the ferns,
　With the look of a human face.

They wove a pillow to symbol her rest,
　And starry gems for her crown,
And lined with blossoms the chamber dim,
　Where we laid her tenderly down.

The air was heavy with fragrance, born
  Of the wealth of the summer's bowers,
But the fairest rose was the rose we hid
  Deep under the mound of flowers.

The blossoms will perish, their petals fall,
  Their sweetness will wither away,
And never a hint of their beauty remain,
  Through the glare of the midsummer's day.
They came in their freshness to comfort our hearts,
  For a moment to brighten the sod,
Our rose was transplanted; forever to bloom,
  In the beautiful garden of God.

RECOGNITION.

THE winter night was dark and chill,
  The wind, through leafless trees,
Swept wildly over vale and hill,
  To moan on lonely seas.

A freighted bark slipped from life's shore,
  Out on an ebbing tide,
The boatman with the muffled oar,
  Companion was and guide.

Companion to the pure, sweet soul,
  Who left her house of clay,
In darkness, for the welcome goal
  Of everlasting day.

O'er seas of space they sped afar,
  No map hath shown us where
The Islands of the Blessed are,
  But they found harbor there.

And mid the throng who came to greet,
  Was one most fair and bright,
With radiant face serenely sweet,
  And eyes of tender light.

Who welcomed with a joyous cry,
  The friend of other days,
Recalling scenes of years gone by,
  With words of love and praise.

And hand in hand they passed along
  That City's streets of gold,
Together sang the glad new song,
  As once they sang the old.

Together climbed the holy heights,
  And plucked the fadeless flowers,
Immortal joys and pure delights,
  Which bloom in heavenly bowers.

And laid their trophies at His feet,
  Whose priceless love had given,
An earthly life, with joy replete,
  And made them heirs of Heaven.

VICTORY.

I THOUGHT thine was the victory, oh, grave!
  And thine the bitter sting, oh, death!
When unto thee my own beloved gave
        Her parting breath.

I saw thee as a monster rude and grim,
  Who tore life's dearest ties apart,
But then, alas! mine eyes with tears were dim
        And sad my heart.

How could I, in that dreadful hour, behold
  The radiance on thy wings of light?
To me thy visage was most stern and cold,
        And dark as night.

But now I know that Christ had conquered death,
  And won a glorious victory,
" The ressurection and the life," He saith
        "Are found in Me."

'Twas but a gentle angel whom he sent,
  From pain my darling to set free;
The grave was but the open way they went,
        With Christ to be.

And when my work is done and I shall go
  To share that blessed eternity,
My loved, with outstretched hands, will smile, I know,
        And welcome me.

"DEAD, YET SPEAKETH."

WITH quiet hands and sealed lips
  Upon the bier she lay,
Still as the form the sculptor moulds
  And fashions from the clay.

Yet not a score of years had left
  Their touch on brow or cheek,
No furrows worn by time or tears,
  Of sorrows seemed to speak.

In life's glad morning she had heard
  The summons from on high:
"Come up, thine earthly work is done:
  Come dwell above the sky."

And death's pale angel hovered near
  Her trembling soul to guide,
When pain had loosed the silver chord
  And love's sweet bands untied.

With patient heart and perfect trust
  In Him who died to save,
She brightened all the dreary way
  Which led her to the grave.

Pain poured for her the bitter cup,
   She drank it with a smile.
Which told of hidden peace and rest
   On God's strong arm the while.

Nor did her faith or patience tire
   By long night-watches tried,
While closer crept the icy waves
   Of Jordan's swollen tide.

The valley dark, no shadow cast,
   'Twas lit by heavenly love;
From sunshine here her spirit passed
   To perfect light above.

Does not the brief, but earnest life,
   The peaceful, happy death,
Say to the listening ear more sure
   Than words of idle breath:

" Live for that life which lies beyond,
   That when its doors swing wide,
God's angels good, may lead thee on,
   Where love and joy abide."

Do not the dead lips seem to say
   In admonition still:
" Be faithful to life's sacred trust
   And do thy Maker's will."

OUR BROTHERS.

WHEN Slavery's oligarchy reared
   Its cruel standard high,
And Treason's blood-red banner flamed
   Across the Southern sky,
And war's shrill tocsin rent the air
   And filled our hearts with dread,
Our brothers heard the trumpet peal,
   Which on to victory led.

In peaceful homes, where plenty smiled,
   And love the board had spread,
They heard their country's call, " to arms, "
   And forth to battle sped.
The farmer hastened from his field,
   The lover from his bride,
The merchant left his counting-house,
   The boy his mother's side.

Through toilsome marches day by day,
   By long night-watches tried,
In camp, in prison, on the field
   They struggled side by side.
A common purpose made them one,
   A common hope they shared,
Resolved their country to sustain—
   For any fate prepared.

Of all who went, but few returned,
   The path to glory led
Through seas of blood, and all the way
   Was strewn with heaps of dead.
Some fell in battle, some in camp
   By grim disease were slain,
And some in Southern prison pens
   Dragged out their days of pain.

But not in vain they suffered, fell,
   The land for which they died,
United, free, will ever be
   The patriot's joy and pride.
In the great camping-ground of all,
   Their "low, green tents" are seen
And ours the holy task shall be,
   To keep their memory green.

Still year by year the summons comes
   To join that silent band,
For living comrades, here and there,
   Wide scattered o'er the land.
For living comrades who still share,
   Their country's hard won peace,
As maimed and battle scarred, they wait
   Their papers of release.

We drop a tear, as one by one,
   Their absence me deplore;
We know the ranks will soon be fiilled
   Upon the other shore.

We know that other hands must guard
    The treasures they have won,
And other feet, more swift and strong,
    Their country's errands run.

Eternal vigilance, is still
    The price of liberty,
And they who guard our country's weal
    Must ever watchful be.
For ignorance, anarchy and crime,
    Are foes which lurk within,
And shameless vice walks hand in hand
    With drunkenness and sin.

That nation only can be great,
    Whose people serve the Lord—
The firm foundation of whose faith
    Is built upon His Word.
For right must triumph in the end,
    And Truth and Virture be
The bulwark of our nation's strength,
    The safeguards of the free.

TEMPERANCE POEMS.

THE MAELSTROM.

FROM the rugged coast of Norway,
　　A gallant ship sailed forth,
Full rigged, with streaming pennons,
　　She turned her prow to the north.
She rounded the headland safely,
　　Swept out on a silver tide—
From the deck, her brave commander
　　Beheld with an air of pride,

How fair was the golden morning,
　　How bright was the shining sea,
No storm-ripple stirred the waters,
　　No whisper of danger to be—
On shore were the green, waving forests,
　　With singing birds, busy and bright,
And the glad, blue heavens were bending
　　Over all, with their smiles of light.

'Twas a joyous bridal party,
　　Who sailed, that summer morn,
And their songs, and shouts of laughter,
　　From deck to deck were borne.
White hands a farewell waving
　　To answering hands on shore,
And the jest and music blending
　　In the merriest uproar.

They sailed, and the fresh breeze freshened,
    The white waves tossed their spray
Like diamonds in the sunshine,
    To speed them on their way.
While the dancing feet flew gaily
    To music's happiest spell,—
O'er the heart of the brave commander
    A sudden terror fell.

" How strangely the water ripples
    Around the vessel's keel,
What means this hidden currant,
    This motion which I feel ?
Port, port your helm," he shouted,
    " Be quick, to larboard tack,
Down hard your helm, for Heaven's sake
    The ship is off her track! "

The sailors read the danger,
    And flew at his command,
The helmsman, though his cheek grew white,
    Bore down with heavy hand.
Well might the captain shudder,
    Well might they tremble all,
For the ship obeyed no rudder,
    Held in the Maelstrom's thrall.

Drawn in those outer circles,
    Inexorable as fate,
They only learned their danger
    When knowledge was too late.

Ah! me, what pen can picture
  The terror and the gloom,   '
When fell upon those happy hearts,
  The certainty of doom!

The same clear sky bent o'er them,
  So pitilessly blue,
The same glad birds were singing
  The forest arches through.
Their own bright homes lay smiling,
  Along the landscape fair,
Its peaceful beauty mocking
  Their agonized dispair.

Round and still round they hastened,
  Fast and yet faster flew,
As nearer to the vortex's mouth
  The dizzying circles drew—
Wild prayers for pardoning mercy,
  From lips unused to pray,
And tears and lamentation,
  Marked all the fearful way.

At last, the ship plunged madly—
  Her creaking masts o'er thrown,
And then the seething, yawning gulf
  Received her as its own.
One shriek from many voices,
  Lost in the whirlpool's roar,
A hopeless struggle with the waves,
  A plunge and all was o'er.

I saw a good ship sailing
　Upon Time's silvery sea,
Full-rigged for Life's long voyage,
　Hope's pennons streaming free.
Childhood's and Youth's glad morning
　Was bright with birds and flowers,
And Joy and Mirth went dancing
　Through all those sun-bright hours.

I saw this gallant vessel
　Speed on her prosperous way,
Reason, the brave commander,
　Rejoicing with the gay—
Will held the rudder lightly,
　But saw no danger near,
And steered upon the crested waves
　Without a thought of fear.

I saw a fearful whirlpool,
　Whose outer circles crept
Unseen, beneath the channel
　This stately vessel swept.
At first, so slight the motion,
　It seemed like Pleasure's swell,
But from the opening vortex gleamed
　The seething fires of Hell.

I saw the good ship reeling
　And tossing on this tide—
In vain the captain shouted,
　In vain the helmsman tried.

Too strong for such weak rudder,
   The hastening current drew
To swift and sure destruction,
   The ship and all her crew.

Friends called a tender warning,
   The shore was still in view,
And Childhood's peaceful harbor
   From whence her anchor drew.
But on, still swifter onward,
   Drawn by that potent spell,
The breeze but wafted backward
   Hope's bitterest farewell.

Through ever-narrowing circles
   Lured to its final goal,
Till from the blackened depths uprose
   The cry of a lost soul!
How terrible the picture!
   Is there no hand to save,
No bow of promise, which man pays
   Across a Drunkard's grave?

Surely as draws the Maelstrom
   Within its fatal snare,
The stately vessel, round and round
   To meet destruction there,
So surely does Intemperance,
   Lure with its poisoned breath,
The noblest intellects of earth,
   To sin and shame and death.

Not one, but many, thousands,
  This mighty whirlpool ends—
Year after year the wrecks go down
  In sight of home and friends.
In sound of warning voices
  Which call along the shore,
" Beware the fatal current,
  Beware the Maelstrom's roar! "

THE HIDDEN SERPENT.

WEARIED and thirsty, from the chase,
  Once rode the Persian king,
And longed for a refreshing draught,
  From out some mountain spring;
Beside him on a halberd perched,
  His well trained falcon rode,
And through the long and tiresome way
  The dusty dragoons strode.

What was it trickling down the cliff,
  And sparkling in the sun?
The precious drops of liquid light
  Were gathered one by one,
And when the golden cup was filled,
  (Which many a banquet graced)
The monarch lifted with a smile,
  The cooling draught to taste.

But suddenly the falcon stretched
   Her dark wings, strong and wide,
As if in rude unconsciousness,
   And dashed the cup aside.
The earth absorbed the waters, which
   The Persian monarch craved,
And treasure gained for kingly lips,
   The weeds and tall grass laved.

Thrice was the golden goblet filled,
   Though slowly, to the brim,
And dashed aside, ere yet the king
   Had touched its jewelled rim.
Then blazed his anger fiercely forth
   And with a cruel blow,
He swore revenge by all the gods,
   And laid the falcon low.

The henchman climbed the rocky cliff,
   In haste the draught to bear,
But shrieked, and fled in horror from
   The sight which met him there,
For lo ! a monster serpent lay
   Coiled in the crystal well,
Whose poisonous venom, filled with death
   Each sparkling drop which fell.

How many, like the Persian king,
   Clasp eagerly the cup
Which holds a poisonous beverage,
   In haste to drink it up;

And scorn the friendly hand which strives
　　To dash the cup aside,
Or turn from friendship's kind appeals,
　　In bitterness and pride;

But learn by sad experience,
　　How like an adder's sting,
Or like a serpent's deadly bite,
　　Is the accursèd thing.
Whoever tastes, will drink again,
　　With thirst beyond control,
'Till poisened by the liquid fire,
　　Are body, mind, aud sonl.

THE PITCHER-PLANT.

BOYS, do you know where a curious plant
　　Called the pitcher-plant is found?
Its ball-shaped flowers of a dark red hue
　　Are seen above marshy ground.
On long, green stems these singular flowers
　　Hang nodding to and fro,
But the strangest part of the plant is seen
　　In the broad, green leaves below.

In the shape of a vase or pitcher they rise,
　　On the top is a well-formed lid,
And down in the depths of each funnelled cup
　　Is a strong, sweet nectar hid.

On sunshiny days they are opened wide
  To lure the unwary flies,
But the sides of the chalice are lined with hairs,
    And whoever enters dies.

So smooth and soft is the downward way,
  None dream of imprisonment near,
Till they seek to return, when those pendant hairs
  As bayonets bristling appear.
But bright in the sunshine it nods its head,
  And never a struggle it heeds,
For day after day this remorseless plant
  On the life of its victim feeds.

Is there not a stranger and sadder sight,
  Whose sign on our pathway is flung,
All gilded and painted in colors bright,
  A snare for the feet of the young?
The drinking saloon has an open poor,
  And lures with its poisonous breath;
Tobacco and beer are the downward way,
  And the end is a drunkard's death.

LOST LAMBS.

"MY lamb, oh where is my one lost lamb?"
   Said a mother-sheep, one night,
     "He has gone astray,
     He has lost his way,
And my heart is wild with fright.

" Has he wandered off on the mountain lone,
   In the woods to starve and die?
     Is he spent with pain?
     I have called in vain,
And I can not hear his cry.

" Have the wild beasts torn him limb from limb ?
   Has he died without a sign?
     I am all alone,
     And my heart makes moan
For this litle lamb of mine.

" Oh where is our guardian, tried and true,
   Who watches with sleepless eyes?
     In the twillight dim,
     Has the wolf met him,
And captured him by surprise?"

Nay, strong and fleet were the gray wolf's feet,
　And his mouth had a bloody stain,
　　　With the watch dog near
　　　He had cause to fear,
　But alas! for the lamb was slain.

"My boy, my boy," said a mother fond.
　"Oh, where is my boy, my pride?
　　　Temptations meet
　　　On the crowded street,
　And their doors are open wide.

" They will lure him into the paths of sin,
　With honeyed words they greet,
　　　With the gilded sign
　　　And the flowing wine,
　They haste to ensnare his feet! "

O guardians of the public weal,
　Who tarry through greed of gain,
　　　Will ye longer sleep,
　　　While the mothers weep,
　And the precious lambs are slain?

THE END THEREOF IS DEATH.

"I WILL have wealth," said a robber bold,
  "I know where the banker stores his gold,
And the key to his strong room now I hold."

He wended his way with a cautious tread,
Nor wakened the sleeper overhead;
To the door of the massive vault it led.

The lock was intricate, strong and rare,
He had learned its secret spring with care,
For he was a trusted servant there.

But love of gold and the greed of gain,
Had bound his soul with a sordid chain,
Till truth and honor alike were slain.

In silence parted the wall of stone,
The massive door was open thrown,
And the robber stood within, alone.

What wealth of treasure greeted his sight,
Of gold which shone with a yellow light,
And many a diamond flashing bright.

He stooped to gather the precious store,
And heeded not when the iron door
Swung noiselessly to its place of yore.

He sought in haste to gather them all,
And feared lest a single jewel fall,
And sighed that his basket was so small.

Then turned, with his treasure to depart,
And paused, with a sudden, fearful start,
And a sickening terror at his heart.

For he was a prisoner, safely bound
By the walls of stone, which girt him round,
And the secret spring its place had found.

He knew, in an instant, his dreadful doom,
He saw how the sides of that narrow room,
Had encircled him in a living tomb.

In his purposed flight he had pondered o'er
The days which would intervene before
The banker would open the iron door.

That chance of safety was now his knell,
He knew the dead, in each narrow cell,
Might look for rescue or help as well.

Why dwell on the horror that waited there,
The frenzied shriek, or the dumb despair,
The muttered curse, or the whispered prayer?

Enough, that only a corpse was found,
With gold and jewels scattered around,
And broken and crushed on the dungeon ground.

"I will have pleasure," a young man said,
"I love the wine when it sparkles red,
It warms my heart and it clears my head."

He knew where wisdom her treasures stored,
And love her jewels for him outpoured,
He thought to gather the precious hoard.

He counted on learning, and length of days,
On fortune's smiles, and the meed of praise,
And worldly honors in various ways.

But gradually round him chains were thrown,
More hopeless than any walls of stone,
And the links were forged by his hand alone.

But fold on fold, and around and around,
Like a serpent's dreadful coil it wound,
Till he was a prisoner firmly bound.

The end was terror, and pain, and woe,
Aye, such as the drunkard alone may know,
Ere he slips to the yawning gulf below.

MISCELLANEOUS POEMS.

THE BEAUTIFUL.

THE stars in their orbits all were set,
 The night had been followed by day,
And earth, from the wildest chaos sprung,
 In its gloomy grandeur lay.

The spirit of Beauty lowly bent
 Before her Creator's throne,
And breathed the wish of her loving heart,
 In a supplicating tone.

"Go," said her gracious Lord, " I give
 Full power to thy fairy hand,
On earth, or sea, or air, to leave
 The touch of thy magic wand."

The spirit sped on her wings of light,
 And crossing the sun's bright ray,
She gave a gorgeous gleam of gold
 To the mighty monarch of day.

Then out in the arching sky, she hung
 A veil of the softest blue,
And over the trees and herbs she flung
 Their own peculiar hue.

She stooped to paint, 'twas a task of love,
  Each tiny floweret's cup,
And a gem of dew, like a radiant pearl,
  In its petals folded up.

Above the cataract's awful brow,
  She bent the Iris bow,
And snowy foam, and a sea-green hue,
  She gave to the depths below.

And over the ocean lingered long,
  To color its thousand waves;
And painted the lips of moaning shells
  Half-hidden in coral caves.

A veil of moss on the brown rock threw,
  And taught the mountain stream
To wind, like a thread of silvery light,
  The bare wild cliffs between.

Thus sped the sprite on her joyous task,
  'Till in cave, or grot, or dell,
No place on the whole broad earth is found,
  Where the beautiful doth not dwell.

THE MOUNTAIN STREAM.

FROM mountain springs, through valleys fair
    A little streamlet ran,
Where flowery banks and fields of green,
    Made glad the heart of man.

In singing mood it hurried on,
    A rover wild and free,
Impelled by force of strong desire
    To seek the distant sea.

Through forests dark, by waving ferns,
    Its devious pathway led,
And sad winds moaned amid the pines,
    As onward still it sped.

Grim mountains at each other frowned
    O'er rocks of granite gray,
But through the defile at their feet,
    The streamlet wound its way.

Birds dipped their golden wings within
    Its waters pure and bright,
And paused, a grateful song to sing,
    Before they took their flight.

The wild deer of the wooded hills,
   'Mid crag-cliffs brown and bare,
Would toss their antlered heads, in haste
 · The cooling draught to share.

From bubbling springs and falling showers,
   The stream still gathered strength,
And grown a river, broad and deep,
   Men's burdens bore at length.

A mart of trade, a great highway,
   The river soon became;
A blessing to the world at large,
   And bore an honored name.

The longing of the mountain stream
   Impelled the river on,
Till, folded in the ocean's waves,
   Its goal at last was won.

OLD AND NEW.

I AM not dead, I can not die
   The old year whispered with a sigh—
I pause to write a deathless name,
Sometimes with joy, sometimes with shame,
Upon the waiting scroll of fame,
And when I turn again to you,
Ye look, and nod, and call me new.

Perchance you saw me as I passed
Storm-girt upon the Wintry blast,
Or marked me, garlanded with flowers,
While resting through the drowsy hours,
In lovely summer's rosy bowers.
But when I garnered in the grain,
Ye watched me, with a thrill of pain.

Ye watched, and murmured with surprise,
"Alas! how soon the Old Year dies!
Why will he never longer stay?
Another may not be as gay,
Another may not come our way,
But he was bright and full of cheer
Why does he hasten to his bier?"

Kind friends, it may be you have heard,
Through ancient lore of fabled bird,
Which from its ashes gayly springs,
To spread anew, exultant wings,
And of the past and future sings—
So I, who meet you with new face,
Still clasp the old in my embrace.

Another name, another age,
I set on history's open page,
Another-tablet pure and white
I offer you, where on to write
Your name in characters of light.
But Time and I are one, and we
Shall die but in Eternity.

SUNSET AMONG THE HILLS.

UPON the summit of a rocky hill I stood,
    Behind me, rose a dark, impenetrable wood,
Around, beneath, in sunset splendor lay
The varying landscape, stretching far away
To hills of purple glory, on whose top
The clouds their silken fringes seemed to drop;
The church-spire, of a little hamlet, towered afar,
As if expectant, waiting for the evening star
To mirror in its polished shaft, her smiling face
And lend to crudest art a welcome touch of grace.

Farm houses dotted, here and there, the verdant plain,
And corn-fields yellow with the harvest's ripening grain,
And orchards bending low beneath their fruitful load,
Skirting the white line of the winding sandy road.
Cattle were grazing in uncounted meadow-lanes,
Whose verdure had been freshened by the recent rains.
Staid oxen, haply ready for the butcher's stall,
And patient kine who listened for the milk-maid's call.
Some drowsy sheep lay stretched along a sun-lit hill,
While half-grown lambs were busy with their gambols
      still.

The forests, touched by frost, a wealth of splendor bore,
Clad in the gorgeous dyes the summer rainbows wore,
Mantles enwrought with crimson, gold and dun,
And every intermediate shade, blended in one.

The chestnut trees had dropped their precious burdens
    down,
And as reward for toil, each wore a golden crown.
From a gnarled oak, whose branches made safe covert
    nigh,
A speckled hawk peered at me, with enquiring eye,
As if he questioned by what right I made my own
The sacred solitude which girt his sylvan throne.

Far to the South the dim line of the ocean lay,
Blent with the sky, as hazy, mystical and gray,
While shapeless masts, and ship-like clouds, together
    seemed to ride
Sometimes along the sky, and sometimes on the tide.
Already in the East, the moon revealed her face,
Pallid and ghost-like, with a shadowy tint of grace,
But in the West, the sun still ruled, with kingly sway,
Uuquestioned Lord of Light, and Monarch of the Day,
Throned on his fiery car, whose brightness over-cast,
The broad arch of the heavens with splendor as he
    passed.

From the horizon to the zenith, fold on fold,
Lay the great crimson clouds, whose borders, touched
    with gold,
Sent back a softened radiance, streaming far and wide,
And to the dying day, a lengthened life supplied.
Slowly down dropped the sun behind the Western hill,
Seeming to pause a moment, peering backward still
Above the hill-tops, to behold with wondering eye,
The fading glory, of his track along the sky,

Flashing to the far East, one swift-expiring beam,
Which lighted up anew each valley, rock and stream,
Then hid his face, that weary sons of toil might rest,
And distant lands by his awakening smile be blest.

From off the painted sky soon faded, one by one,
The ever-varying dyes, and shapes, wrought by the sun,
The gold grew dim, the crimson changed to gray,
Form after form, of wondrous beauty, passed away,
And soon the twilight shadows o'er the lancscape fell,
Veiling the mountains brow, hiding the mossy dell,
The brief, chill, autumn twilight, passing swiftly by,
For moon and stars to light again the evening sky.

And even thus, I thought, the good man sinks to rest,
Like suns which set in splendor, leaving earth still
    blessed,
Not lost in gloom, but wrapped in glorious light,
And leaving far behind, a path-way pure and bright.
A life whose holy influence dies not with the day,
A memory whose radiance fades not soon away.
And even thus the soul, death hides from mortal sight,
Dies not, but like the sun, still treads a path of light,
And other lands grow bright, and other spirits own
The sun whose warmth and light we have so fondly
    known.

SPRING-TIME.

A GLIMMER of wings in the air,
    A ripple of song in the wood,
A flush of pink on the orchard bare,
    And the spring-time sweet and good.

Spring with its violets blue,
    Its dandelions of gold,
Its daisies in ruffles white and new,
    And its snow-drops pure and cold.

With crocuses yellow and gay,
    And the blood-root pale and fair,
And ferns, with heads all frizzy in May,
    And the song-birds everywhere.

The spring with its fresh delight,
    In tears and in laughter now,
But stretching hands full of blossoms bright,
    To scatter on every bough.

This life has its spring-time fair,
    Its April of smiles and tears,
Its treasures of beauty with naught of care,
    And joy in the passing years.

The spring is the seed-sowing time,
    The farmer must scatter the grains,
Adapting his seed to land and clime,
    And planting with thought and pains.

Life's seed-sowing time is in youth,
   Then faithfully plant while you may,
The harvest of growing error or truth,
   Be sure you will gather some day.

KING WINTER.

AWAY in the North, lives the old Winter king,
   And strange though it seems he is next door to
       Spring,
His palace of ice is most fair to behold,
And gleams in the sunlight more brilliant then gold.

One day to the queen, said King Winter, "I hear
That Autumn is late about moving, this year,
I wish he would pack up his trappings and go,
The children I'm sure must be wishing for snow.

" 'Tis time that my annual journey was taken,
And all the dead leaves from the forests were shaken,
'Tis time that the brook and the stream by the mill
Should hush up their babbling awhile and keep still.

"I have sent the first frosts, by lightning expressed.
My blizzards already are packed for the West,
I have in my satchel a North-wind or two,
O'er which the good people will make much ado.

" The children are ready with mittens and sleds,
And warmest of caps for their dear little heads,
They do have such sport when I cover with snow,
The hill from its top to the valley below.

" I know the old people will shiver and shake,
And say that one-half of their comfort I take,
But children will never grow rosy and strong,
If I keep my good breezes away from them long.

"So I must be off, in a hurry, my dear,
For Christmas is waiting for me with New-Year,
They're merry companions, we'll travel together,
And care not a fig for the coldest of weather."

THE MISSING GUY.

HOW tall and straight the smoke-stack rose
    A hundred feet in air,
Upreared with anxious thought by those
    Who fashioned it with care.
More slowly now, almost in place—
    The tall top bends and sways—
With bated breath the strain we trace
    Along the lengthend stays.

Another inch and firmly held,
    The shaft for years will stand.
By wind and storm in vain repelled,
    A land-mark in the land.

But see, it topples, it will fall,
    The bottom guy is where?
A little strength, a child's, quite small,
    Might save, expended there.

Alas! the rope was missing there—
    A moment still and slow
Like a long pendulum hung in air,
    The shaft swung to and fro;
Then with a heavy crash, it fell
    A shattered, ruined mass,
And crushed and broken fragments tell
    Of ruin where it passed.

Have you not seen a shapely life
    Rise stately, tall, and fair,
With intellectual grandeur rife,
    And fashioned well with care?
Almost in place, it seems to be,
    We scarcely mark it swing,
Till suddenly, instead, we see
    A wrecked and ruined thing.

In searching for the cause of all,
    The missing guy we trace!
A single cord had saved the fall,
    If fastened at the base.
Anchored to Christ, the cord of love
    Had held through trial's strain,
Temptation sought in vain to move,
    Or sin the soul to stain.

THE MAGDALEN.

"Behold I stand at the door and knock."

'TWAS a woman young and fair
 Peering through the lattice oft
At the busy thoroughfare.
  She was robed in raiment soft;
There were jewels in her hair.

But a look of guilt and pain
 Shone from out the bold, dark eyes,
You could read the sin and stain
 Through the glittering disguise,
Wealth had spread for her in vain.

In her pure and happy home,
 'Mid the granite hills afar,
E'er her feet had learned to roam,
 Shone her beauty like a star.
Ah! why did the tempter come?

But amid the crowd that day,
 Who swept past her gilded cage,
Came a form more bowed and gray
 With heart-sorrow than with age.
Was it chance that led that way?

Nay, for at the door he stood
        Knocking long, and knocking loud :
Not like beggar seeking food
        Seemed his form amid the crowd,
Looked his face so pure and good.

And her cheeks grew white with pain,
        As she watched him with surprise,
And a sudden dash of rain
        Dimmed the brightness of her eyes—
But the knocker knocked in vain.

And again, and yet again,
        Through the long and weary day,
'Mid the jostling crowd of men,
        Came the patient one that way,
Though he knew the noisome den.

He had traced his lost one there,
        And he hoped to see her face,
While he thought his pleading prayer
        Might yet win her from the place,
But he only found despair.

And his bitter grief she read,
        As she watched him, o'er and o'er,
And she bowed in shame her head;
        But she would not ope the door,
"I have chosen this " she said.

But through all the livelong day
      Knocked another at her heart,
While she would not bid him stay
      Still reluctant to depart,
Though she whispered, "go thy way."

When the midnight shadows spread,
      She yet heard his still, small voice,
As she tossed upon her bed,
      "I have made a wretched choice,"
In her bitterness she said.

"To my father's house, once more,
      Let me haste to rise and go,
On my mother's bosom pour
      All my guilt and shame and woe,
While there waits an open door."

Through the darkness which had been,
      Shone the light of dawning day,
From the heart all stained with sin,
      Fell the bars and bolts away,
And the Crowned One stood within.

MEMORIES.

L ET me think of pleasant fields to-night,
    Where my feet in childhood strayed,
Of the low, green hills, with daisies white,
    Where a band of children played.

Of the shallow brook which murmured low,
    And its waters pure and sweet,
Where we drank from leafy cups of green,
    Or we splashed with bare brown feet.

Of the quaint old barn, with cosy nooks,
    And its odorous new-mown hay,
Where we used to climb the ladders tall,
    And at hide and seek, to play.

Of the shady woods, so cool, near by,
    And the berries red and sweet,
Of the wintergreen we used to pick,
    With the beech-nuts 'neath our feet.

Of the luscious draughts of sweet we sipped,
    In the merry, sugaring time,
When the maples rang with laughter peals,
    Like a great bell's joyous chime.

For we could not guess in those bright years,
    Of the changes time would bring,
To the unfledged birds, in that home nest,
    Beneath love's sheltering wing.

We are scattered all, we wandered far
    Away from those hills of green,
And the finger-marks of time and care,
    Upon every brow are seen.

But some sleep near, where moonlight soft
    Its silvery mantle spreads,
And the daisies white and butter-cups,
    Are nodding above their heads.

And although we tarry a little while,
    Wherever our feet may roam,
We know, that the paths in which we walk,
    Will certainly lead us home.

GRATITUDE.

IN a home of wealth and beauty
  Where the golden sunlight strayed
Through the heavy silken curtains,
  Over frescoed walls, and played
On the forms of marble whiteness,
  Which the sculptor's hand had wrought,
And illumined rarest paintings,
  From most ancient cities brought—

'Mid the softness and the splendor,
  Of those wondrous works of art,
Sat the fair and gifted owner,
  With a discontented heart.
She had love and youth and beauty,
  Troops of friends on every side,
But her snowy brow was clouded,
  For some fancied bliss denied.

Should the song bird she had chosen,
  To another nest have flown?
Should the jewel she might covet,
  On another's breast have shone?
Should there aught but good be gathered
  In that rich and ample fold,
Where were genius, culture, station,
  Blent with fashion, wit and gold?

From her heart no prayer ascended,
  From her lips no song of praise,
For the blessings round her clustered,
  For the brightness of her days!
Though her cup ran o'er with mercies,
  And her life was free from care,
It had no room for thankfulness,
  And gratitude no share.

In a low and dingy cabin,
  With its bare, unpainted walls,
Through whose narrow, broken windows
  The Autumn sunlight falls—
Sits a feeble, lonely widow,
  Who is poor and old and blind,
Sometimes ill and sometimes hungry,
  Oft neglected by her kind.

Day by day goes by in darkness,
  Night by night comes on alone,
Saving only for His presence,
  Who yet hears the feeblest moan,
Of the humblest of his creatures,
  And in tender love draws near,
Dispelling by his brightness
  All the loneliness and fear.

Is there room for thoughts of mercies,
  Is there place for words of praise,
In a life which seems so barren?
  "God is good to me," she says,

" Every day he feeds and clothes me,
　And his faithful care displays
Through his ministering servants,
　In a thousand kindly ways,

" All these years, his hand has led me,
　And the blessed peace I share
Through the brightness or the darkness,
　Helps me all my burdens bear ;
Though I know not, what the future
　Hath reserved for me so late,
Still I know, God will not fail me,
　I can trust him while I wait."

Thus it is not wealth or station,
　Not the things we have and hold,
Which makes the germ of gratitude,
　To perfect flower unfold.
But the heart that sees the giver,
　In the bounties of his love,
And knows that 'mid all changes,
　His mercies changeless prove.

HENRY OF NAVARRE.

THUS wise and brave was Henry of Navarre,
Who led the Protestants in holy war.
    Halting the troops who fled
    Appalled before the dead,
    Which blocked their onward way,
    At Ivry, one sad day.

"Nay, brothers, nay, ye need not fight," he said,
"But each one toward the battle turn his head.
    And linger ere ye fly
    Until ye see me die."
    Then swiftly far ahead
    His white plume glancing led.

Thrilled with a quick, responsive sympathy,
The brave men followed, ready each to die,
    The lost field soon was won,
    And ere the setting sun,
    Triumphant rang the cry,
    Of " France and victory."

THE EMPTY NEST.

FAR from the noisy village street
    Within the green wood's cool retreat,
Where stately trees their branches spread,
To weave a canopy o'erhead,
And trailing vines and mosses hung,
By idle zephyrs gently swung,
And all the air betokened rest,
A shy bird built her quiet nest.

But not alone, for with her flew
Her faithful mate so fond and true,
And in and out with nicest care
They wove the tiny strands of hair,
With slender grasses, reeds and straw
And lined the whole without a flaw,
A home for sweet content it seemed,
Of home-like happiness they dreamed.

And soon beneath the downy breast,
Four fragile eggs were gently pressed,
And watched and guarded night and day,
And warmed and brooded o'er alway.
And day by day the wonder grew,
The waxen, mottled spheres of blue,
Were filled with vague and strange unrest,
For life was hovering o'er the nest.

A murmur of imprisoned things,
The quivering of unseen wings,
And lo! the palaces so fair
Lay crushed, four gaping mouths were there,
Oh! then with swift and joyous wing,
From far and near the food they bring,
And flutter o'er the birdlings there,
With eager, fond, parental care.

Was it some woodman's axe which brought
Destruction to the home unsought?
Some careless hunter's idle shot
Which reached that fair, sequestered spot?
Some boy on cruel mischief bent?
Some prowling beast with foul intent?
It boots not, since the mother found
Her callow brood, dead on the ground.

Poor mother bird! thy little breast
Hath room for that unwelcome guest,
Who finds a place in hut and hall
And brings a bitter cup to all.
Hast thou no dream of coming spring
Wherewith to soothe thy sorrowing?
No resurrection morning when
Thy loved ones thou shalt meet again?

God pity those who everywhere
A load of hopeless sorrow bear,
Who look not through the prison bars
To life and love beyond the stars.

For such, the only boon to bless,
Must be a bird's forgetfulness,
Who plucks the feathers from her breast
To build anew the ruined nest.

WIND FLOWERS.

ON wide, far-stretching plains,
    Where Cacti most abound,
A species singular and rare,
    Of this strange plant is found.

When winds are hushed and still,
    And skies serenely fair,
The bristling, scraggy objects stand,
    Devoid of grace and bare.

Their leaves are pale and gray,
    Set round by thorny spears,
Nor hint of hidden bud or bloom,
    Along their stalks appears.

But when a rude gale shakes
    The plants, with fury bold,
From waiting, undiscovered buds,
    A thousand flowers unfold.

Large, creamy white, and pure,
    Waked by the tempest's breath,
They flutter while the strong wind blows,
    Then sleep in seeming death.

And there are human lives,
    As bare and blossomless,
Sunned by prosperity and peace,
    Hedged round by selfishness.

They wait for sorrows touch,
    Their stubborn hearts to move,
For strong winds of adversity,
    To open flowers of love.

JOSEPH'S TOMB.

IN the fertile valley of Shechem,
    Where Ebal's shadow falls,
And Gerizim (mount of blessing)
    Looks down o'er rocky walls.
Hemmed in by the cloud-capped mountains,
    'Neath ever changing skies,
Alone in the valley of beauty
    The tomb of Joseph lies.

He fell in the land of Egypt,
    And centuries passed by,
While in faith his bones were resting
    Beneath that alien sky.

He said, " Ye shall surely bear me
  Out to that goodly land
Which was promised to our fathers—
  Led by God's mighty hand."

But the freighted years rolled onward,
  And through their music crept
The bitterest plaint of sorrow,
  The voice of them that wept.
For "the new king knew not Joseph,"
  Nor the people whom he fed,
And through cruel persecutions
  Their path to freedom led.

In the hurry of swift departure,
  And through their devious way,
Over sea or the trackless desert,
  They bore the coffined clay.
Till they reached the land of promise,
  With fertile fields of green,
Where they made in that lonely valley
  The grave which faith had seen.

We, too, have a land of promise,
  A land so fair and bright,
In visions of wondrous beauty
  It flashes on our sight.
And ever, as on we journey,
  Faith points that heavenly way,
Where death and its gloomy shadows
  Are lost in endless day.

THE OLD CANNON.

L OW down among the reeds and rushes,
   Hidden half by weeds and bushes,
      Grim relic of a bitter day—
A day, when neath the shot and shell,
The soldiers like the mown grass fell—
      An old deserted cannon lay.

A cannon, which, in time of war,
Had sniffed the battle from afar,
      And foremost in the dreadful fray,
Its volleys poured, of flame and death,
While heroes yielded up their breath,
      Throughout that long and painful day.

But in the marshes stranded fast,
Wrecked, and abandoned there at last,
      For long years rusting it had stood,
While winds of summer round it blew,
And bending branches o'er it threw
      The dancing shadows of the wood.

At length, one sunny morn in May,
A pair of thrushes passed that way,
      In search of some sequestered spot,
Wherein to build their downy nest,
And, of its narrow walls possessed,
      To be by ruder birds forgot.

How silent seemed the sylvan shade,
Where gleams of sunshine softly strayed,
　　How peaceful looked the ruin there,
Fit place to build a home of love,
Abode for e'en the gentle dove,
　　So thought and wrought the happy pair.

And thus, from out the jaws of death,
Awoke at last, life-giving breath,
　　And sweetest songs of praise and joy,
Foreshadowing that time of peace,
When war shall cease, and love increase,
　　And men no more God's gift destroy.

And often from the ponderous wheel,
The thrush poured forth his joyous peal,
　　Resounding through the leafy glen,
In melody like that which stirred
The ancient shepherds, as they heard
　　The song of "Peace, good-will to men."

THE PRAYER-MEETING.

THE snow lay white on wooded hill,
    And white on valleys low,
In silence slept the frozen rill,
Whose waters fed the fulling mill
    In summers long ago.

But from the old church belfry tower
    A chime rang bravely out,
To tell of an appointed hour
Of worship, and to rouse with power
    The people far about.

Peal upon peal, and clang on clang,
    Out on the frosty air
The brazen tongue its message sang,
And through the leafless branches rang
    The welcome call to prayer.

From near and far they gathered fast,
    O'er fields of trackless white,
Unmindful of the biting blast,
Or feathery snow-flakes hurrying past,
    Like swallows in their flight,

Through winter's cold or summer's heat,
    Alike, they heard the bell,
And thither came with willing feet,
The "old, old story," to repeat
    And God's great love to tell.

Warm hearts and earnest souls had they,
    That rugged path who trod,
And little children left their play
To hear their fathers praise and pray,
    And learn through them of God.

Young men and maids found there the way,
    Regardless of the weather,
So mixed life's motives, who shall say
If love of God, or man, held sway,
    The homeward path together.

That life, at least, is well begun,
    Commenced in wisdom's ways.
Continued thus, till set of sun,
The Master's plaudit of "well done"
    Will crown its closing days.

The plain old church has passed away;
    A grander one is there,
With gilded spire and windows gay,
And furniture in bright array;
    Whose bell still calls to prayer

And young and old together meet,
  Triumphant songs to raise.
And still, in conversation sweet,
The " old, old story " they repeat,
  And give to God the praise.

THE SNOWBIRD.

A WILD storm of winter swept over the land,
  The North Wind laughed loud in his glee,
And he tossed the snow-drifts like billows of sand
  Cast up by the tempest-wrought sea.

He shook the tall trees of the forest, which stood
  With their branches all leafless and cold,
And twisted and rent the frail saplings of wood,
  With the oaks of a century old.

As I watched from my window, all sheltered and warm,
  The drifts which went hurrying by,
A poor little snowbird, half dead in the storm,
  Attracted my wandering eye.

So beaten about by the pitiless blast,
  So helpless and chilled was the bird,
With feathers all rumpled, and spirits downcast,
  My heart was with sympathy stirred.

I saw how he sought for some remnant of food,
    As he paused on the desolate plain,
Where dry, blackened stalks of the past summer's weeds
    Gave faint promise of gathering grain.

But no morsel of seed, to reward him at last,
    To the dry, scentless, herbage could cling,
And the storm, on swift pinions, swooped down as it
      passed,
    And bore him aloft on its wing.

Where, whirled for a moment, he hung in mid-air,
    Benumbed by the hunger and cold,
Then dropped on my casement, all helpless to bear
    Still longer his trials untold.

Then I opened my window with welcoming hand,
    And drew the poor wanderer home
To a snug little basket, so warm, on my stand,
    To wait till the sunshine should come.

There the warmth and the shelter, the rest and the food
    Soon brightened the storm-beaten bird,
And I fancied, he strove to give thanks for the good,
    In the faint, little chirpings I heard.

And I thought of the Father, whose pitying love,
    The fall of the sparrow doth heed—
With tender compassion he hears from above
    The cry of each soul in its need.

I thought of the arms of his mercy, wherein
    The tempest-tossed spirit may hide,
Of the dear, loving Savior, the refuge from sin,
    Where comfort and safety abide.

THE HOUSEHOLD PET.

WE have a little favorite
    The sweetest of all things,
Should you see her, you might call her
    A cherub without wings,
Or a fairy, bird, or blossom,
    You may call her what you will,
For to each she bears resemblance,
    But herself is better still.

Her hair is soft and golden,
    As the petals of a flower,
Her eyes like blue forget-me-nots,
    In summer's brightest hour.
Her voice is low and joyous
    As the carol of a bird,
Her step, like rustling blossoms
    By evening zephyrs stirred.

Her motions are the fairy's,
    So full of witching grace,
And you read her guileless nature
    In the sunshine of her face.

A pretty April blossom,
 A bright bird of the wild,
A fairy or a cherub,
 She yet is but a child.

And she plays the "Grandma" nicely
 With her dolly by the fire ;
Is the idol of her aunties
 And the treasure of her sire—
And she knits and sews demurely
 As any olden dame,
Or at least, pretends to do it,
 Which is very much the same.

You should see our little baby,
 In her robe of snowy white,
As she steals about on tip-toe,
 To kiss us all good-night.
Should see her clasp her dimpled hands
 Beside her little chair,
And with tongue which falters often,
 Lisp out her evening prayer.

You should see—but I'd forgotten
 It is only "our sweet pet,"
To others, but a common child
 To glance at, and forget.
A child, a free, glad-hearted child
 Has earth a thing more fair ?
Holds heaven a richer treasure
 Than the bright ones gathered there ?

THE BELL OF JUSTICE.

IN an old Italian city,
    In the grand square once was hung,
Without steeple, tower, or belfry
    To impede its brazen tongue—
A great bell, whose noisy clanging
    Could be heard from far and wide,
As it echoed through the valleys
    And along the mountain side.

It was called the Bell of Justice,
    For the grand old judge had said,
" Let it swing where all the people
    Can behold it overhead;
Are there any wrongs unrighted,
    Aught of justice in demand,
Let the old bell tell the story,
    Let it sound it through the land.

" Let the great bell tell the story,
    If the poor have been oppressed,
If the greed of men, or malice,
    Any helpless have distressed,
I will hasten at its summons
    All your burdens to make light;
And the rouges shall all be punished,
    And the wrongs shall be made right."

So the bell its summons sounded
   And the years flew on apace,
And the ends of justice failed not
   In that law-abiding place.
And the rope grew worn and broken
   Swinging idly in the wind,
And at last a thrifty grapevine
   With its strands were intertwined.

Then one day the judge was startled,
   Such a sharp appeal to hear,
Clang on clang, the old bell sounded
   Out its message loud and clear.
And the judge assumed his ermine
   With his retinue of-state,
And went forth to meet complainants
   Who might for his presence wait.

But he saw not man nor woman
   In the great square, far or near,
Nor the voice of those who wrangled
   Nor lamented, smote his ear;
But a horse, both old and hungry,—
   Scarred by many a cruel blow,
Feeding meekly on the grapevine,
   Swung the old bell to and fro.

When the judge beheld the creature,
   With a grave, judicial air,
As a minister of justice,
   He this sentence did declare:—

"Thus the court decrees,—Your owner
   Shall, from this time onward, feed
And shelter you in kindness,
   According to your need.

"And the cruelty which will not
   For such faithful servant care,
Shall be punished with imprisonment,
   And stripes a liberal share."
Then the herald, with his trumpet,
   Blew a long, triumphant blast,
And the judge and his attendants
   From the Court of Justice passed.

THE KING'S REPLY.

THE English monarch, George the Fourth,
   Was riding out one day,
In Windsor Park, with prancing steeds
   And carriage bright and gay.
He met a coarse and blustering man,
   Who thought it very wise
To flaunt his scorn of royalty,
   Before the monarch's eyes.

"Uncover, 'tis the King we meet,"
   Said one who rode anear,
"Your disrespect will be construed
   As anarchy, I fear."

The fellow answered with an oath
  We would not dare repeat,
"I'll not take off my hat to him,
  Or any king I meet."

The King, who heard the rude remarks,
  Replied, with gracious smile,
And bowed with stately courtesy
  And lifted hat, the while.
"I to my meanest subject would
  This much of honor give,
And pray that long and happily
  The gentleman may live."

The King passed on, the subject paused,
  Surprised to thoughtfulness—
Was he indeed the gentleman
  Who practiced gentleness?
Would courtesy and kindliness
  As truly honor bring,
And dignify the humblest man
  As though he were a King?

THE ROMAN MOTHER AND CHILD.

INTO the great Cathedral stole,
  To pray for peace to her husband's soul,
A Roman matron fair and mild,
And in her arms she bore their child.

The huge, bronze statue of the great
St. Peter sat enthroned in state,
Still gravely offering one toe
For kisses from the throng below.

The Roman mother lowly bowed
Amid the sanctimonious crowd,
And pressed her lips with fervent zeal,
Which good St. Peter well might feel.

Then softly bent the golden head,
" Kiss it, Petruchio," she said,
" The good St. Peter ne'er will bless,
If we neglect this kind caress."

The youthful Roman tossed his curls,
And glancing toward the baby girls,
But touched the bronze, as if to say,
" 'Tis only that I must obey."

Then with a sudden, joyous shout,
He flung his little arms about
A living cherub by his side,
Who to escape him, vainly tried;

And kisses pressed, a perfect storm,
Upon her cheek so soft and warm,
In token of his loving heart,
And nature's triumph over art.

The smiling crowd with nod and beck,
As loth the pretty scene to check,
Slowly dispersed, and went their way,
Before some other shrine to pray.

But some, more thoughtful, bore away
In troubled consciences that day,
The questions: " Wherefore should we kneel
To forms which neither see nor feel?

" Why should we hope for blessings thrown
From folded hands of sculptured stone,
From hearts which neither throb nor move,
While God and Christ still live and love?

"Why should we tell to saints our needs,
Since Christ for us still intercedes?
He holds the key all keys before,
And opens wide the heavenly door."

THE BLESSING.

"GIVE us this day our daily bread,"
    With lisping tongue the baby said,
And clasped her dimpled hands the while
She bowed her head with trusting smile,
And asked His blessing, who alone
Has power to guard and keep His own.

Above the music of the spheres
Whose rapture fills unending years,
Amid the sound of angel bands,
Who chant His praises, harp in hand,
Blent with the songs of seraphim,
The prayer of childhood rose to Him.

Its guileless trust, in sweet accord
With angels' and arch-angels' word,
Its love as pure, its faith as strong
As that which winged the seraph's song.
Distinct and clear, through paths unknown,
It reached the Father's ear alone.

In swift response the blessing came
The bread and meat were still the same,
But better than the choicest food,
The spirit's peace, the inward good,
The kinship with the Holiest
That made the heart of childhood blest.

Oh! Love Divine, which stoops to bear
The burdens of our earthly care,
Which watches o'er our daily needs,
And still the waiting spirit feeds
On bread of life, whose rich supply
The soul that eateth, shall not die.

THE OLD YEAR.

WHAT has the old year brought
    Save weariness and care,
The year which dawned so bright,
    With promises so fair?

What record has been borne
    Across the silent sea,
Where garnered stores from time
    Await eternity?

Some change in every life,
    A year for young and old,
Some cherished dreams have flown,
    Some friendships have grown cold,

Some loss of confidence
    And trust in human good,
Where still the wise are weak
    The best misunderstood.

Some homes made desolate
   By death's relentless hand,
Too oft the vacant chair,
   The broken household band.

But mid the wrong and ruth,
   Some better things appear,
Something undying, brought
   By the poor, dying year.

For those who fell asleep,
   Rest from all earthly pain,
While love assurance gives
   For them " to die is gain."

Have not the living plucked,
   Along the thorny way,
Some bright, unfading flowers,
   Too precious for decay?

A firmer faith in God,
   As human friends have failed,
And brighter hopes beyond,
   As earthly joys have paled.

The strength endurance gives,
   The peace which follows pain,
The joy of sacrifice,
   Some greater good to gain.

A deeper consciousness,
   Though all things else may fail,
That truth and righteousness
   Shall in the end prevail.

That God, unchangeable,
  His purpose doth fulfill,
Through us, or over us,
  According to our will:

Through us, when willingly
  We walk in wisdoms ways,
Though e'en the wrath of man
  Shall manifest his praise.

We greet thee then, Old Year,
  Hail, and farewell, to thee!
May other years still bring
  Our ships, from o'er the sea.

Our ships, with treasure filled,
  Whose worth, time can not tell,
We wait eternity,
  Till then, Old Year, farewell.

THE BRIGTH SIDE.

LOOK on the bright side, 'tis ever the right side,
  Doubt and discouragement conquer no foes,
Some clouds will gather in all sorts of weather,
  From springs early dawning, to stern winters close.

'Tis the sunshine with showers, which awakens the flowers,.
  And labor will strengthen the sinews of youth,
Through the black cloud is shining a bright silver lining,
  And victory rides on the banner of truth.

Little skill on the wave, would the mariner have,
  If storm-ripples never disturbed the blue sea,
But the good ship must ride through the stormiest tide,
  And ruler and lord of the tempest must be.

Though a shadow may fall, on our pathway so small,
  Shall we think the whole universe shrouded in night?
While the smoke dims our eyes, far up the blue skies
  The sun and the stars shine eternally bright.

To look moodily down, to murmur or frown,
  Will make neither burden nor sorrow more light,
The golden-hued morning, the green hills adorning,
  Will dawn on the longest and dreariest night.

When shines on our vision the sweet fields elysian,
  Where Love and Peace dwell, with no fears to annoy,
What we, in our blindness, called Heaven's unkindness,
  Shall crown us, immortal, with beauty and joy.

HARVEST HOME.

(SONG.)

FROM summer's dusty toil
　　We tillers of the soil
With sheaves have come—
Bringing blest autumn's dower,
Of richest fruit and flower,
For this triumphant hour
　　Of Harvest Home.

From farm or shop or mill
Our busy hands we fill
　　With trophies rare—
To tell of harvests stored,
Of industry's rich hoard,
By plenty's hand out-poured,
　　And God's good care.

The swiftly passing year
Has brought us health and cheer
　　And joy and rest;
Plague has no terrors hurled,
And war's red flag is furled—
At peace with all the world—
　　Our homes are blessed.

Our father's God, and ours,
For sunshine and for showers

We praise Thy name!
May blessings from Thy hand
Still fall, like grains of sand
Upon the ocean strand,
    Ever the same.

As year shall follow year,
May we assemble here,
    Crowned with Thy love,
Till, earthly labor done,
And all time's triumphs won,
Beyond life's setting sun,
    We meet above.

LITTLE KATHERINE.

AWAY in the north of Russia,
    It is bitterly cold you know,
They have long and tedious winters,
    With heaps upon heaps of snow.

They muffle themselves in bear skins,
    And wrap up the children in furs,
And then, in the stormiest weather,
    There's scarcely a creature stirs.

But ever the days of sunshine
    Will follow the days of storm,
And over the gleaming snow-fields
    The sun shines brightly and warm.

They harness the dogs for horses,
　　And sometimes the swift reindeer,
Enjoying a merry sleighride
　　With never a thought of fear.

The people are brave and hardy,
　　The children are rosy and bright,
Who work with a will when needful,
　　Or play with a child's delight.

They chatter and talk in a language
　　Which few of us understand;
But dimples and tears and laughter,
　　The same are in every land.

A hut, in a great, and lonely forest,
　　Was where little Katherine lived,
Her father and brothers were hunters,
　　And fishermen, too, who thrived.

Her brothers were strong and manly,
　　As rugged as mountain pine,
And Katherine fair as the blossom
　　Which brightens the clinging vine.

A sun-shiny day for the hunters
　　To follow their winding way.
A busy work-day for the mother,
　　Left Katherine free to play.　'

She gathered her treasures together,
　　And out in a wide, sunny space,
Warmly wrapped, with her sled and her shovel,
　　She found a most beautiful place.

She fashioned a curious snow-man,
  She rode down the steep hillside,
And wonderful snowballs, unnumbered,
  She rolled in a heap with much pride.

And when the brief day was declining,
  She caring no longer to roam,
Sought the pathway she trod in the morning,
  Which led to her own quiet home.

But devious paths by the hunters
  Bewildered the poor little maid,
The faster she sped through the forest,
  The further from home she had strayed.

And soon on her path fell the shadow
  Of trees which their long branches tost,
The way had grown wilder and rougher,
  And Katherine knew she was lost.

She ran and cried out in her terror,
  She sobbed out each dearly loved name,
Alone in the cold and the darkness,
  But no one to rescue her came.

Her mother at home, growing anxious,
  Had called and recalled from her door,
Then hastened to search in the places
  Where Katherine lingered before.

The danger increased with the darkness,
  For many a ravenous beast
Lay hidden all day in his covert
  Awaiting the night for his feast.

The hunters came weary and laden
　　With bear's meat and skins, quite a store,
But hastened away with their torches,
　　Their hearts beating heavy and sore.

They called, and they searched all the by-ways,
　　Could little feet travel so far,
O'er rough paths and no paths, unaided,
　　Unguided by moon and by star?

At last, the long search was rewarded,
　　When hope for the moment had fled,
One cried out for joy as he stumbled
　　Above a small shovel and sled.

Farther on, in a den with some bear cubs,
　　Whose mother the hunters had slain,
Safe and warm, little Katherine rested,
　　In slumber forgetting her pain.

www.ingramcontent.com/pod-product-compliance
Lightning Source LLC
Chambersburg PA
CBHW020111030726
47498CB00006B/2052